I0745996

Nomad

The Miracle of Minerals: Discovering the Circuit Makers of Our Inner Self

NoMAD

The Miracle of Minerals: Discovering the Circuit Makers of Our Inner Self

Copyright © *Levitas One*, 2024
All Rights Reserved

This book is subject to the condition that no part of this book is to be reproduced, transmitted in any form or means; electronic or mechanical, stored in a retrieval system, photocopied, recorded, scanned, or otherwise. Any of these actions require the proper written permission of the author.

What are the NoMAD Plans?

Developed by Dr Ash Kapoor, the NoMAD Plans represent a transformative approach to health and wellness that combines the wisdom of ancestral practices with contemporary medical insights. The name "NoMAD" not only suggests a journey through the intricate realm of health but also stands for its foundational principles: Nutritional Optimisation, Mindful Adaptation, and Detoxification.

At the heart of NoMAD is the 6R Framework—Restore, Release, Repair, Renew, Reframe, and Represent. This methodology addresses the root causes of illness, combats chronic inflammation, and cultivates authentic vitality, guiding individuals through a transformative process.

Tailored specifically to each individual, NoMAD journeys are meticulously crafted to rebalance the body, strengthen the mind, and rejuvenate overall health. By integrating ancestral practices with cutting-edge, innovative treatments—all under strict medical oversight—NoMAD Plans offer a personalised pathway to sustainable, long-lasting well-being that resonates with your unique life circumstances.

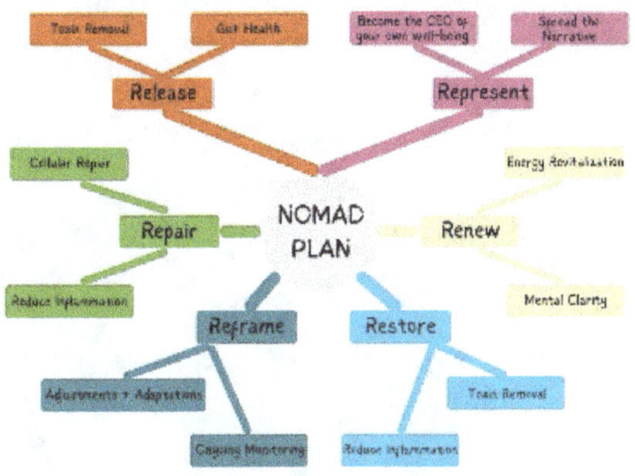

Levitas One:
"As Is In, As Is Out"

Reflecting the belief that our internal well-being is mirrored in our external environment. Founded by Dr. Ash Kapoor, Levitas One serves as the vehicle for delivering NoMAD's treatment plans. It envisions a healthcare future where patients are at the centre of a fully integrated, multidisciplinary approach. Guided by Nomads 6 Rs— Restore, Release, Repair, Renew, Reframe, and Represent—Levitas One empowers self-care through personalised guidance and minimal intervention, promoting long-term health, balance, and sustainability.

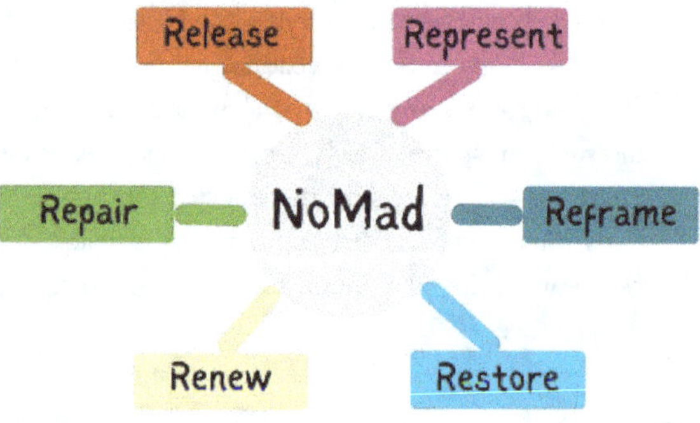

Contents

Preface

Having spent the majority of my career in the conventional medical world, I realised how little advice or knowledge is given about the critical role minerals play in health. This oversight has been a missed opportunity, as something as simple as mineral replenishment can dramatically improve people's lives. Sadly, the depletion of minerals in our soils has rendered much of today's produce suboptimal in nutritional value, leaving many individuals deficient in essential nutrients without even knowing it.

Our ancestors did not face these issues. They sourced their minerals naturally from their environment, through mineral-rich water, unprocessed foods, and soils that were not yet depleted by modern agricultural practices. Today, we face a new challenge—one that demands restoration therapy to address these mineral gaps in our diets and lives. Restoration therapy can help fill this void, allowing us to optimise our health, prevent chronic diseases, and improve overall well-being.

In this book, I hope to provide healthcare professionals and readers with the knowledge to navigate the complex yet vital world of minerals. These nutrients are the "circuit makers" in our bodies, driving energy production, brain function, immune health, and much more. By reclaiming the power of minerals, we can restore our health from the inside out, just as our ancestors once did—only now, we must be intentional about it.

It is my hope that the insights shared here will help guide both professionals and readers alike toward a healthier future through the essential wisdom of mineral replenishment.

— Dr. Ash Kapoor

Regenerative Physician

Introduction
The Forgotten Foundation of Health

Minerals are the unsung heroes of human biology. While vitamins, proteins, and fats often take centre stage in discussions of nutrition and health, minerals work quietly in the background, supporting virtually every biochemical process in the body. From muscle contractions and nerve signalling to hormone production and DNA synthesis, minerals play a foundational role. Yet, despite their critical importance, they are often overlooked in modern healthcare. In today's fast-paced world of processed foods, over-farmed soils, and filtered water, mineral deficiencies are alarmingly common—so common, in fact, that many people are unaware that they may be living in a state of chronic mineral depletion, contributing to a host of health problems that could easily be avoided with proper attention to this often neglected aspect of nutrition.

The Overlooked Importance of Minerals

In the world of biochemistry, minerals are essential elements, meaning the body cannot synthesise them. They must be obtained through diet or supplementation. Calcium, magnesium, potassium, iron, zinc, and selenium are just a few of the many minerals that support life, each with its own set of crucial functions. For example, calcium is best known for its role in maintaining strong bones, but it also plays a critical role in muscle function, blood clotting, and nerve transmission. Magnesium is another multitasker, involved in over 300 enzymatic reactions in the body, from energy production to regulating blood sugar levels and maintaining healthy blood pressure.

Despite their essential roles, minerals often do not receive the attention they deserve. Part of this is due to their invisibility; we can feel the immediate effects of low energy when we lack carbohydrates or protein, but the effects of mineral deficiencies tend to be subtler and more insidious, building up over time. Fatigue, brain fog, brittle bones, irregular heartbeat, weakened immunity, and even anxiety or depression can all be symptoms of mineral deficiencies. Yet, they are often attributed to other causes, leading to treatment that ignores the root issue.

Why Minerals Are Essential

The human body requires minerals to perform a wide range of physiological functions. They are integral to the formation of bones and teeth, the proper functioning of muscles and nerves, the synthesis of hormones, and the regulation of fluid balance in the body. Minerals are also critical for enzyme function—without them, the body's metabolic processes would come to a grinding halt. This means that without sufficient minerals, the body's ability to produce energy, repair tissues, regulate blood sugar, and even maintain mental health is compromised.

Consider iron, for example. This mineral is a critical component of haemoglobin, the protein in red blood cells responsible for carrying oxygen from the lungs to tissues throughout the body. A deficiency in iron leads to anaemia, a condition that can cause extreme fatigue, shortness of breath, and cognitive impairments. Similarly, magnesium deficiency can lead to a wide range of health problems, from muscle cramps and irregular heartbeat to anxiety and sleep disturbances. Despite these obvious signs of deficiency, minerals are rarely given the spotlight in discussions about health and nutrition.

The Shift Away from Mineral-Rich Diets

Historically, humans obtained minerals in abundance from their diet. Early hunter-gatherer societies ate a varied and nutrient-dense diet rich in plants, wild game, and fresh water, all of which provided an abundant supply of essential minerals. Even as societies transitioned to agriculture, the soil remained rich in nutrients, and water sources provided trace elements that supported optimal health. Traditional diets also included mineral-rich sea salts, like Celtic salt, which supplied not just sodium but also magnesium, potassium, and trace elements like iodine, which are vital for thyroid function and metabolic health.

However, modern dietary habits have shifted away from this mineral-rich foundation. Processed foods, stripped of their natural nutrients during manufacturing, now dominate the global food supply. Industrial farming practices, which rely on monocropping and chemical fertilisers, have depleted the soil of its natural mineral content. As a result, even fresh fruits and vegetables today contain far fewer minerals than they did a century ago. At the same time, water filtration systems, while crucial for removing contaminants, also strip water of beneficial minerals, such as magnesium and calcium.

The shift to highly refined table salt, devoid of the trace minerals found in natural sea salts, is another contributing factor. Refined salt consists almost entirely of sodium chloride. In contrast, natural salts like Celtic salt contain a wealth of other minerals, including magnesium, potassium, and trace elements like zinc and manganese, which support immune function, nerve transmission, and bone health.

The Health Impact of Mineral Deficiencies

The consequences of mineral deficiencies are far-reaching. Modern diseases such as osteoporosis, cardiovascular disease, diabetes, and even mental health disorders have all been linked to chronic mineral deficiencies. For example, magnesium deficiency is associated with an increased risk of heart disease, type 2 diabetes, and hypertension. Zinc deficiency weakens the immune system, making individuals more susceptible to infections and slowing wound healing. Calcium deficiency, especially in older adults, leads to bone density loss and increases the risk of fractures.

While these deficiencies are often subtle, they can have a profound impact on health over time. A person with a mild magnesium deficiency, for instance, may experience occasional muscle cramps and fatigue, but as the deficiency worsens, more serious issues like arrhythmias (irregular heartbeats) and chronic fatigue may develop. Similarly, a zinc deficiency may first manifest as frequent colds or slow wound healing but can progress to more severe immune dysfunction or cognitive decline if left untreated.

The Forgotten Heroes of Health

Despite the growing body of evidence linking mineral deficiencies to a wide range of health issues, minerals are still often overlooked in both public health discussions and individual treatment plans. This is partly due to a focus on macronutrients (carbohydrates, proteins, and fats) and vitamins, which are more easily understood and marketed. There is also a misconception that minerals are only needed in tiny amounts, and thus deficiencies are unlikely. However, while it is true that many minerals are needed in trace amounts, even small deficiencies can lead to significant health problems over time.

Another challenge is that mineral deficiencies often mimic other health conditions. For example, fatigue and cognitive difficulties, common symptoms of both iron and magnesium deficiencies, are often attributed to stress, ageing, or sleep disorders. As a result, many people suffering from mineral deficiencies may be misdiagnosed or treated with medications that do not address the root cause of their symptoms.

Reclaiming Health Through Mineral Replenishment

The good news is that mineral deficiencies are relatively easy to correct with the right approach. For many, the first step is simply being aware of the problem. By reintroducing mineral-rich foods into the diet—such as leafy greens, nuts and seeds, seafood, and whole grains—people can begin to replenish their mineral stores. In some cases, supplementation may be necessary, especially for those with absorption issues or higher-than-average needs, such as athletes or individuals with chronic health conditions. For more severe deficiencies, intravenous (IV) mineral therapy offers a direct route to replenishment, bypassing the digestive system and ensuring rapid absorption.

Minerals may be the forgotten foundation of health, but their impact is undeniable. As we continue to navigate the complexities of modern living, from dietary challenges to environmental stressors, reclaiming our health through mineral replenishment offers a simple yet powerful solution. By bringing minerals back into the spotlight, we can address the root causes of many common health problems and build a stronger foundation for long-term well-being.

Conclusion

Minerals are the cornerstone of human health, essential for the proper functioning of every cell, tissue, and organ in the body. Yet, they have been largely overlooked in modern healthcare, leading to widespread deficiencies that silently undermine health. As we become more aware of the critical role minerals play in our well-being, there is an opportunity to correct this imbalance and restore vitality. Whether through diet, supplementation, or advanced therapies like IV mineral drips, the key to better health may be simpler than we think: a return to the forgotten foundation of health—the minerals that support life itself.

Summary: Introduction
The Forgotten Foundation of Health

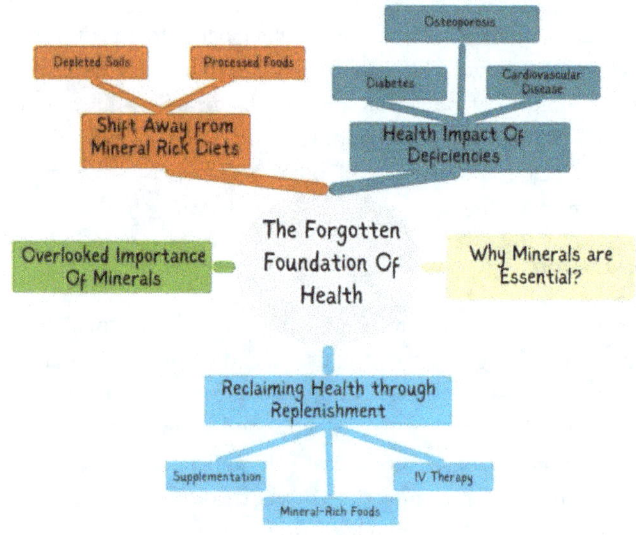

Chapter 1
How Our Ancestors Thrived with Natural Mineral Intake

Minerals, in their most natural forms, were once abundant in the daily lives of our ancestors, contributing to their physical vitality, cognitive strength, and overall well-being. Long before modern agriculture and industrialised food production, people sourced their nutrition directly from the earth—eating wild plants, hunting animals, drinking fresh spring water, and relying on the mineral-rich soils that nourished their food. This chapter explores the richness of ancient diets, the connection between natural food sources and essential minerals, and the practices that enabled our ancestors to thrive in environments that supplied them with these vital nutrients.

Mineral-rich Diets of Ancient Societies

As mentioned earlier, long before the advent of modern agriculture, human diets were largely shaped by the environment. Hunter-gatherer societies, which existed for tens of thousands of years, relied on a diverse array of wild plants, fruits, nuts, seeds, and animals to meet their nutritional needs. These foods, untouched by processing or refinement, were naturally abundant in essential minerals.

Hunter-Gatherer Diets

Hunter-gatherers consumed a varied diet that included nutrient-dense plants, fruits, seeds, and animal products. These wild foods were often higher in minerals than today's processed foods. For example, wild game meat, such as deer or elk, contains higher levels of zinc and iron than farm-raised meat. Additionally, wild plants, grown in untamed soils, were packed with a variety of essential nutrients like magnesium, potassium, and calcium. The soil in which these plants grew had not yet been depleted by industrial farming, ensuring that crops retained their natural mineral content.

Foraging for nuts, berries, and roots also contributed to a highly mineral-rich diet. Nuts like walnuts, almonds, and hazelnuts provided essential minerals like magnesium, manganese, and copper. These were critical for metabolic functions, energy production, and the maintenance of strong bones and muscles. Leafy greens, which are rich in calcium and magnesium, were also a significant part of the hunter-gatherer diet, and wild tubers like yams and sweet potatoes provided ample potassium to maintain fluid balance and support cardiovascular health.

In terms of animal products, the consumption of organ meats such as liver and kidneys—foods that are incredibly dense in iron, zinc, and copper—was commonplace among hunter-gatherers. These meats, revered for their nutrient density, were often eaten first after a successful hunt, reflecting an intuitive understanding of their health benefits.

Early Agricultural Societies

As humans transitioned from hunter-gatherer societies to early agricultural systems, diets shifted but continued to be rich in essential minerals. Early farmers relied on diverse crops, including grains like barley, millet, and wheat, alongside legumes such as lentils and peas. These foods were often consumed whole, retaining their natural mineral content.

The soil in early agricultural societies had not yet been exhausted by monocropping and synthetic fertilisers. As a result, it was rich in minerals like selenium, magnesium, and calcium. Farmers practised crop rotation and other techniques that maintained the mineral integrity of the soil. This practice ensured that foods grown in these regions were packed with essential minerals necessary for maintaining health and vitality.

Additionally, early agricultural societies maintained a connection to wild food sources. For example, many Mediterranean civilisations supplemented their agricultural diets with seafood, a rich source of iodine, magnesium, and selenium. This combination of cultivated and wild foods provided a broad spectrum of minerals, ensuring that early agrarian societies continued to meet their nutritional needs.

Water and Soil: Nature's Mineral Delivery Systems

In ancient times, natural water sources like rivers, streams, and springs played a crucial role in providing essential minerals. Unlike today's purified and filtered water, which removes many naturally occurring minerals, ancient water sources were rich in magnesium, calcium, and trace elements such as selenium and silica. People consumed water directly from these sources, benefiting from the minerals dissolved in the water as it flowed over rocks and soil, which naturally infused it with these life-sustaining elements.

Mineral-Rich Soil

Soil, too, was a critical source of minerals for ancient peoples. The soils in which plants grew had not been depleted by overfarming or exposed to chemical fertilisers, both of which strip the land of its mineral content. The soil was replete with magnesium, calcium, and other trace minerals. Plants absorbed these minerals through their roots, and humans obtained them by consuming both the plants and the animals that fed on them.

Ancient agricultural practices, such as allowing fields to lie fallow and using composted organic matter to enrich the soil, helped maintain the mineral integrity of the land. This ensured that the crops, fruits, and vegetables grown in these early societies provided the essential minerals necessary for human health.

Ancestral Practices for Mineral Replenishment

In addition to sourcing minerals from food and water, ancient cultures had specific practices that helped them maintain optimal mineral levels. Indigenous practices across the globe demonstrate a deep understanding of the importance of consuming mineral-rich foods, salts, and natural supplements to promote health and vitality.

Foraging for Wild Foods

Foraging was a critical part of the ancestral diet, and it brought people into direct contact with foods that were naturally abundant in minerals. Indigenous peoples across the world knew which plants, berries, roots, and mushrooms provided essential nutrients, including minerals. For example, seaweed, consumed by coastal communities, is rich in iodine, magnesium, and calcium. In traditional Japanese and Inuit diets, seaweed has long been used not only as food but also as a natural remedy for iodine deficiency, which can cause thyroid problems and metabolic issues.

Consumption of Organ Meats

Ancient peoples placed great importance on consuming the whole animal, especially the organ meats, which are highly concentrated sources of minerals. Liver, for example, is one of the richest sources of iron, zinc, and copper. Indigenous peoples often prioritised organ meats over muscle meat, consuming them immediately after a successful hunt to ensure the best nutrition. This practice was observed among Native American tribes, African hunter-gatherers, and traditional societies in South America.

Sea Salt and Mineral-Rich Salts

Salts, particularly unrefined sea salts like Celtic salt, have been used for thousands of years to enhance both flavour and nutrition. Unlike modern table salt, which is stripped of minerals during processing, Celtic salt and other natural sea salts contain more than 80 trace minerals, including magnesium, calcium, potassium, and iron. Ancient cultures understood the importance of consuming mineral-rich salts. In fact, salt was so valuable in many parts of the ancient world that it was used as currency in trade.

Sea salt was particularly prized in coastal regions of Europe, Africa, and Asia. The ancient Celts harvested salt from the ocean, drying it in the sun to retain its natural mineral content. Similarly, the Egyptians and Greeks relied on sea salt not only to preserve food but also as a vital source of minerals for maintaining health and energy.

Case History: Ancient Egypt and Greece – Strength Through Mineral-Rich Diets

Ancient civilisations like Egypt and Greece were highly attuned to the health benefits of mineral-rich foods. The Egyptians, known for their advanced understanding of medicine and nutrition, incorporated a variety of mineral-dense foods into their diet. Bread made from whole grains, seafood from the Nile, and vegetables grown in the fertile soil of the Nile Delta provided ample amounts of calcium, magnesium, and potassium. Additionally, Egyptians placed great emphasis on the consumption of mineral-rich plant foods like garlic and onions, which were believed to enhance strength and stamina.

Mineral-rich salts, too, were an integral part of Egyptian life. Salt was used not only for preserving food but also for enhancing physical strength and vitality. Athletes and labourers, especially those involved in the construction of the pyramids, were given mineral-rich foods and salts to ensure that they could endure the physical demands of their work.

The Greeks, likewise, understood the connection between minerals and health. They consumed a diet rich in whole grains, legumes, seafood, and leafy greens, all of which provided essential minerals like iron, zinc, and calcium. Greek athletes, in particular, were known to consume large amounts of mineral-rich foods, including figs, olives, and sea salt, to improve their physical performance. The famous physician Hippocrates often prescribed mineral-rich sea water as a treatment for various ailments, recognising its restorative properties.

In both Egypt and Greece, these ancient societies thrived on diets that were naturally abundant in essential minerals, which supported not only their physical strength and endurance but also their intellectual and cultural achievements.

Conclusion: Thriving on Nature's Abundance

Our ancestors had an intuitive understanding of the importance of minerals in their diets, and their practices reflected this knowledge. By consuming whole foods, foraging for wild plants, and using mineral-rich salts, they maintained the essential mineral balance necessary for health and vitality. They lived in harmony with the earth, benefiting from the minerals present in natural water sources, nutrient-rich soil, and the foods they hunted and gathered.

In contrast, modern diets often fall short of providing the necessary minerals due to soil depletion, processed foods, and purified water. As we reconnect with the wisdom of the past, we can learn how to replenish our bodies with the essential minerals that once sustained our ancestors and thrive in a world where optimal health is within our grasp.

Summary: How Our Ancestors Thrived with Natural Mineral Intake

Chapter 2
The Modern Dilemma –
Why We Face Mineral
Deficiencies Today

Minerals are foundational to human health, yet in today's world, mineral deficiencies have become increasingly common. Despite advances in medical science and access to food, we face a paradox: widespread deficiency in the essential nutrients that were once readily available to our ancestors. The shift in how we farm, process food, and live our daily lives has dramatically altered our relationship with minerals, leading to a silent epidemic of mineral depletion. In this chapter, we'll explore the reasons behind this modern dilemma, including industrial farming practices, the effects of processed foods, water filtration, lifestyle stressors, and the far-reaching health consequences of these deficiencies.

Industrial Farming and Soil Depletion

One of the most significant contributors to mineral deficiencies today is modern industrial farming. In the past, agriculture was more localised, and crops were grown in rich, nutrient-dense soils that had time to regenerate naturally. Today, however, large-scale farming operations use intensive methods that deplete the soil of its mineral content without allowing for replenishment.

Monocropping and Synthetic Fertilisers

Monocropping, the practice of growing a single crop year after year on the same land, is common in modern agriculture. While efficient for producing large quantities of a particular crop, this method strips the soil of specific nutrients, including essential minerals like magnesium, zinc, and potassium. Without crop rotation or soil regeneration practices, the soil becomes increasingly nutrient-poor with each harvest.

In an attempt to boost crop yields, farmers often rely on synthetic fertilisers. These fertilisers typically contain nitrogen, phosphorus, and potassium (NPK), the three primary nutrients needed for plant growth. However, they lack the full spectrum of minerals that healthy soil should provide. As a result, while crops may grow quickly and appear robust, they are deficient in the trace minerals that plants used to absorb naturally from the soil. This mineral depletion is passed on to the food we eat, leaving us nutritionally deficient despite consuming the same foods that nourished our ancestors.

Pesticides and Soil Microorganisms

The widespread use of pesticides further exacerbates the problem. Pesticides kill not only harmful pests but also beneficial soil microorganisms. These microorganisms play a critical role in breaking down organic matter and releasing minerals into forms that plants can absorb. When the microbial ecosystem of the soil is disrupted, the availability of essential minerals like magnesium, iron, and calcium is reduced. This means that even when crops are grown in mineral-rich soils, their ability to absorb these nutrients may be compromised due to the destruction of the soil's natural balance.

Processed Foods and Mineral Loss

In addition to industrial farming practices, the modern diet—dominated by highly processed and refined foods—has contributed significantly to the depletion of minerals in our bodies. Processing methods strip foods of their natural nutrients, leaving them calorically dense but nutritionally poor.

Refinement of Grains

One of the most striking examples of mineral loss through processing is the refinement of grains. Whole grains like wheat, rice, and oats are rich in minerals such as magnesium, zinc, and iron. However, during the refining process, the outer layers of the grain (the bran and germ) are removed, and with them, the majority of the grain's mineral content. What remains is the starchy endosperm, which contains far fewer nutrients.

White bread, white rice, and other refined grain products have become dietary staples in many parts of the world, but their consumption can contribute to mineral deficiencies over time. For example, magnesium levels are significantly lower in white bread compared to whole grain bread. Over-reliance on refined grains, combined with the decreasing mineral content in crops, has created a dietary environment where even those who eat regularly may not be getting the minerals their bodies need.

Processed Snacks and Convenience Foods

In addition to refined grains, many processed snacks and convenience foods are low in essential minerals. Foods like chips, cookies, and sugary cereals are often made with highly refined ingredients and lack the naturally occurring minerals found in whole foods. Moreover, these foods are typically high in sodium, which can further exacerbate mineral imbalances by displacing other vital electrolytes like potassium and magnesium.

The increasing reliance on these foods is particularly concerning given their prevalence in the modern diet. Convenience has taken precedence over nutrition, leading to widespread mineral deficiencies, even in populations that appear well-fed.

Water Filtration and Its Impact on Mineral Content

Water is another essential source of minerals, particularly in its natural, unprocessed form. Historically, humans relied on natural spring water, which was rich in dissolved minerals like calcium, magnesium, and potassium. Today, however, water filtration and purification processes—while essential for ensuring water safety— have inadvertently stripped water of many of its beneficial minerals.

Modern Tap Water vs. Natural Spring Water

Modern water treatment plants filter out contaminants from tap water to make it safe for consumption. This process often involves removing harmful bacteria, chemicals, and heavy metals. However, in the quest to purify water, many beneficial minerals are also lost. For example, calcium and magnesium, which are naturally present in hard water, are often reduced during the filtration process. Softened water, while free of contaminants, lacks the mineral content that our ancestors received from drinking natural spring water.

In contrast, ancient spring water was a rich source of these minerals, contributing to the overall mineral intake of people living in those times. Today, bottled mineral water is one of the few remaining sources of naturally mineral-rich water, but it is often not accessible or affordable for everyone. As a result, many people unknowingly miss out on a critical source of minerals that their bodies need for optimal function.

Dehydration and Mineral Imbalance

In addition to the depletion of minerals in drinking water, many individuals do not drink enough water to maintain proper hydration, leading to further mineral imbalances. Minerals like sodium, potassium, and magnesium play a crucial role in maintaining fluid balance in the body. When water intake is insufficient, these electrolytes can become imbalanced, leading to symptoms like fatigue, muscle cramps, and dizziness.

Increased reliance on filtered water and decreased water consumption contributes to a growing imbalance in the body's mineral stores, further exacerbating the issue of modern mineral deficiency.

Stress and Lifestyle: The Hidden Drain on Minerals

Modern lifestyles are more stressful than ever before, and this stress takes a toll on the body's mineral reserves. Stress increases the body's demand for minerals like magnesium, calcium, and potassium, which are required to regulate the nervous system, support adrenal function, and maintain cardiovascular health.

The Role of Magnesium in Stress Response

Magnesium is often referred to as "nature's tranquilliser" because of its ability to calm the nervous system and regulate the body's stress response. During periods of stress, the body uses up magnesium at an accelerated rate. This is because magnesium is required for the production of cortisol, the body's primary stress hormone, as well as for maintaining healthy blood pressure and supporting muscle relaxation.

Chronic stress can lead to magnesium depletion, resulting in symptoms such as anxiety, irritability, and insomnia. The depletion of magnesium also sets off a vicious cycle, as low magnesium levels can make the body more susceptible to stress, further exacerbating mineral imbalances.

Sedentary Lifestyles and Poor Sleep

In addition to stress, modern sedentary lifestyles contribute to mineral deficiencies. Physical inactivity can impair circulation, reducing the body's ability to transport and utilise minerals efficiently. Furthermore, poor sleep quality—often a byproduct of stress—can interfere with the body's natural mineral replenishment processes, particularly magnesium, which is critical for restful sleep.

Health Consequences of Mineral Deficiencies

The widespread mineral deficiencies caused by industrial farming, processed foods, water filtration, and lifestyle stressors have far-reaching health consequences. Deficiencies in minerals like magnesium, calcium, potassium, and zinc have been linked to a range of chronic health conditions.

Anxiety and Insomnia

Magnesium deficiency is strongly associated with increased levels of anxiety and poor sleep. As mentioned earlier, magnesium plays a critical role in regulating the nervous system and promoting relaxation. Low levels of magnesium can make it difficult to manage stress and anxiety, leading to a cycle of poor sleep and heightened stress.

Many individuals who suffer from insomnia or anxiety find that magnesium supplementation significantly improves their symptoms, highlighting the importance of maintaining adequate mineral levels for mental health.

Osteoporosis

Calcium and magnesium deficiencies are primary contributors to the development of osteoporosis, a condition characterised by weak and brittle bones. Inadequate calcium intake leads to reduced bone density, while insufficient magnesium impairs calcium absorption, compounding the problem. The result is an increased risk of fractures, particularly in older adults.

Cardiovascular Disease

Minerals like potassium, magnesium, and calcium are essential for maintaining cardiovascular health. Potassium helps regulate blood pressure by counteracting the effects of sodium, while magnesium supports healthy heart rhythms and prevents arterial calcification. Deficiencies in these minerals can lead to high blood pressure, arrhythmias, and an increased risk of heart attack and stroke.

Weakened Immunity

Zinc and selenium are vital for immune function, and deficiencies in these trace minerals can weaken the body's defences against infections. Zinc is involved in the production of immune cells, while selenium acts as an antioxidant, protecting the body from oxidative stress and inflammation. Without adequate levels of these minerals, individuals are more susceptible to infections and slower to recover from illness.

Case History: The Link Between Magnesium Deficiency and Fatigue

Consider the case of Sarah, a 35-year-old woman who had been experiencing chronic fatigue and difficulty sleeping for several years. Despite trying various diets and exercise regimens, her symptoms persisted. After consulting with a functional medicine practitioner, Sarah's blood tests revealed that she had a significant magnesium deficiency.

Sarah's practitioner recommended that she start taking magnesium supplements and increase her intake of magnesium-rich foods like leafy greens, nuts, and seeds. Within a few weeks, Sarah noticed a marked improvement in her energy levels. Her fatigue lessened, and she began sleeping more soundly at night. Over time, as her magnesium levels stabilised, her overall sense of well-being improved dramatically.

Sarah's case illustrates how something as simple as correcting a mineral deficiency can have a profound impact on health and quality of life.

Conclusion: Addressing Mineral Deficiencies in a Modern World

The modern world presents unique challenges when it comes to maintaining optimal mineral levels. Industrial farming, processed foods, water filtration, and stressful lifestyles have all contributed to the widespread depletion of essential minerals in our bodies. The consequences of these deficiencies are far-reaching, affecting everything from mental health and sleep to bone density and cardiovascular function.

However, by understanding the causes of mineral deficiencies and taking proactive steps to address them—through dietary changes, supplementation, and lifestyle adjustments—we can reclaim our health and prevent many of the chronic conditions that plague modern society. The key is recognising the importance of minerals as the "circuit makers" of our inner selves and ensuring that we give our bodies the nutrients they need to function optimally in today's world.

Summary: The Modern Dilemma – Why We Face Mineral Deficiencies Today

Chapter 3
Understanding the Essential Minerals – Their Functions and Natural Sources

Minerals are foundational to human health, serving as the building blocks for many of the body's critical functions. From muscle contractions to immune defence, minerals play a vital role in keeping our bodies functioning optimally. While modern society focuses heavily on macronutrients (proteins, fats, and carbohydrates) and vitamins, the essential role of minerals is often overlooked. This chapter will explore the key essential minerals, where they are found in nature, and the role they play in maintaining health.

Major Minerals

1. Calcium

- **Function**: Calcium is perhaps the most well-known mineral, largely because of its role in maintaining strong bones and teeth. About 99% of the body's calcium is stored in bones and teeth, where it supports their structure. However, calcium is also critical for muscle contraction, nerve transmission, and blood clotting. It plays a key role in intracellular signalling and enzyme activation, helping cells communicate effectively. Calcium is also necessary for maintaining a stable heart rhythm.

- **Sources**: Calcium is abundant in dairy products such as milk, cheese, and yoghurt. Leafy green vegetables like kale, bok choy, and spinach are also good plant-based sources of calcium. Sardines, with their small, edible bones, provide a rich source of calcium, and certain nuts, seeds, and fortified foods like almond milk and tofu can contribute to calcium intake.

- **Dosage:** The recommended daily intake for calcium is around 1,000 mg for adults, increasing to 1,200 mg for women over 50 and men over 70 to prevent osteoporosis and maintain bone density.

2. Magnesium

- **Function:** Magnesium is involved in more than 300 biochemical reactions in the body, including energy production, protein synthesis, blood pressure regulation, and nerve and muscle function. It helps regulate the contraction and relaxation of muscles and supports a stable heart rhythm. Magnesium is essential for bone health, as it influences bone density by regulating calcium transport and absorption. It also plays a role in blood glucose control and blood pressure regulation.

- **Sources:** Leafy green vegetables like spinach and Swiss chard are excellent sources of magnesium. Nuts, seeds, whole grains, and legumes also provide significant amounts of this mineral. Other good sources include avocados, bananas, and fatty fish such as salmon and mackerel.

- **Dosage:** Adults should aim for 400-420 mg/day for men and 310-320 mg/day for women. Magnesium deficiencies are common due to poor soil quality and dietary habits, and supplementation may be required for many individuals.

3. Potassium

- **Function**: Potassium is critical for maintaining proper fluid balance in the body, as it works alongside sodium to regulate cellular hydration. It also plays a key role in nerve transmission, muscle contractions, and heart health. Potassium helps maintain normal blood pressure by balancing the effects of sodium. A proper potassium intake can reduce the risk of stroke, lower blood pressure, and help prevent osteoporosis and kidney stones.

- **Sources**: Bananas are a well-known source of potassium, but potatoes, citrus fruits, tomatoes, and leafy greens like spinach also provide ample amounts of this mineral. Other good sources include beans, lentils, and certain fish, such as halibut and salmon.

- **Dosage**: The recommended daily intake for potassium is 2,500-3,000 mg for adults. Most people do not meet this requirement due to inadequate consumption of fruits and vegetables, which are rich in potassium.

4. Sodium

- **Function**: Sodium is essential for maintaining fluid balance, nerve transmission, and muscle contraction. It helps regulate blood pressure by controlling the amount of fluid in the blood vessels. Sodium works in conjunction with potassium to ensure that the proper electrical charge is maintained in nerve cells and muscles, enabling them to function correctly.

- **Sources**: Sodium is commonly found in table salt and processed foods. However, it also occurs naturally in seafood, vegetables, and dairy products. While sodium is necessary for health, excessive intake is a common problem, particularly in Western diets, which rely heavily on processed foods.

- **Dosage**: The recommended daily intake of sodium is 1,500-2,300 mg. Consuming too much sodium can lead to hypertension and other cardiovascular issues.

5. Phosphorus

- **Function**: Phosphorus is essential for bone health, as it works with calcium to build and maintain bones and teeth. It also plays a vital role in energy production and the formation of ATP (adenosine triphosphate), the energy currency of cells. Phosphorus is involved in the repair of tissues and cells and plays a part in the formation of DNA and RNA.

- **Sources**: Meat, dairy products, fish, eggs, and legumes are all rich in phosphorus. Nuts, seeds, and whole grains also provide good amounts of this mineral.

- **Dosage**: The recommended daily intake for phosphorus is 700 mg for adults. Deficiency is rare but can occur in cases of severe malnutrition or overconsumption of antacids, which can block phosphorus absorption.

6. Iron

- **Function**: Iron is a key component of haemoglobin, the protein in red blood cells that carries oxygen from the lungs to tissues throughout the body. It also plays a role in energy production, immune function, and the production of certain hormones. Iron is necessary for proper growth, development, and cellular function.

- **Sources**: Red meat is the most well-known source of iron, but lentils, beans, spinach, and fortified cereals are also excellent sources, particularly for vegetarians and vegans. Iron from plant sources is less readily absorbed than iron from animal sources, so consuming it with vitamin C-rich foods can enhance absorption.

- **Dosage**: The recommended daily intake of iron is 8 mg for men and postmenopausal women, and 18 mg for women of childbearing age, who are at greater risk of deficiency due to menstruation. Pregnant women need even more—27 mg/day. Iron deficiency is one of the most common nutritional deficiencies globally, leading to anaemia.

7. Zinc

- **Function**: Zinc is vital for immune function, wound healing, protein synthesis, and DNA synthesis. It also plays a role in cell division and growth. Zinc is crucial for maintaining a healthy immune system, as it supports the production of immune cells that fight infections. Additionally, it influences the function of many enzymes and hormones, including insulin.

- **Sources**: Meat, shellfish, and dairy products are some of the richest sources of zinc. Plant-based sources include legumes, seeds, and nuts, but the bioavailability of zinc from plant foods is lower than from animal products.

- **Dosage**: The recommended daily intake is 8 mg for women and 11 mg for men. Zinc deficiencies are more common in vegetarians, as plant-based diets can reduce zinc absorption.

8. Copper

- **Function**: Copper is important for iron metabolism, as it helps the body use iron efficiently to form red blood cells. It also supports nerve function and collagen production, which is essential for healthy skin, connective tissue, and bone. Copper has antioxidant properties, helping to protect cells from damage caused by free radicals.

- **Sources**: Shellfish, seeds, nuts, whole grains, and beans are all rich in copper. Organ meats like liver are another potent source of this mineral.

- **Dosage**: The recommended daily intake is 900 mcg/day for adults. Copper deficiency is rare but can occur with conditions that affect nutrient absorption.

9. Iodine

- **Function**: Iodine is crucial for the production of thyroid hormones, which regulate metabolism, growth, and development. Without adequate iodine, the thyroid gland cannot produce enough hormones, leading to hypothyroidism or the development of goitres. Iodine deficiency during pregnancy can result in developmental delays and intellectual disabilities in the infant.

- **Sources**: Seaweed is one of the richest sources of iodine. Other sources include fish, dairy products, and iodised salt.

- **Dosage**: The recommended daily intake is 150 mcg for adults. Iodine deficiency is still common in parts of the world where iodised salt is not used, and it remains a leading cause of preventable intellectual disabilities.

10. Selenium

- **Function**: Selenium is a powerful antioxidant that helps protect the body from oxidative stress and supports immune function. It also plays a crucial role in thyroid function by regulating the production of thyroid hormones. Selenium is important for reproduction and DNA synthesis.

- **Sources**: Brazil nuts are an exceptionally rich source of selenium. Other sources include fish, meat, eggs, and whole grains.

- **Dosage**: The recommended daily intake is 55 mcg for adults. Deficiency is rare but can occur in regions with selenium-deficient soils.

11. Manganese

- **Function**: Manganese supports bone formation, amino acid metabolism, and the functioning of enzymes involved in antioxidant defence. It plays a key role in the formation of connective tissue and blood clotting factors. Manganese is also important for brain and nerve function.

- **Sources**: Whole grains, legumes, nuts, seeds, and leafy greens are good sources of manganese. It is also found in tea, which can contribute significantly to daily intake.

- **Dosage**: The recommended daily intake is 1.8 mg for women and 2.3 mg for men. Deficiency is uncommon but can lead to bone problems and impaired growth.

12. Chromium

- **Function**: Chromium is vital for regulating blood sugar levels and improving insulin sensitivity. It enhances the action of insulin and plays a role in carbohydrate, fat, and protein metabolism. Chromium supplementation may improve blood sugar control in people with type 2 diabetes.

- **Sources**: Broccoli, grape juice, whole grains, and meats are good sources of chromium. Some foods, like brewer's yeast, are also rich in this mineral.

- **Dosage**: The recommended daily intake is 25-35 mcg/day for adults. Chromium deficiency is rare but may contribute to impaired glucose tolerance.

13. Molybdenum

- **Function**: Molybdenum is a cofactor for enzymes involved in detoxification and the metabolism of sulfur-containing amino acids. It helps the body break down and eliminate toxins and is involved in the metabolism of drugs and alcohol.

- **Sources**: Legumes, grains, leafy vegetables, and liver are good sources of molybdenum.

- **Dosage**: The recommended daily intake is 45 mcg/day for adults. Deficiency is rare but can result in problems with detoxification and sulfur metabolism.

Trace Elements

Beyond the major minerals, the body also requires trace elements in very small quantities, which play unique roles in maintaining health. Although these elements are needed in minuscule amounts, they are no less important than the major minerals.

- **Arsenic**: At trace levels, arsenic may play a role in the metabolism of certain amino acids, but its precise function in human health remains under study. It is found in seafood, grains, and drinking water in some areas.

- **Rubidium**: This trace mineral may help with maintaining electrolyte balance and cellular energy production. It is found in small quantities in certain vegetables and grains.

- **Strontium**: Strontium supports bone health and mimics calcium in the body. It is found in seafood, whole grains, and leafy greens.

- **Bismuth**: Often used in medicinal compounds, bismuth may support gastrointestinal health by protecting the stomach lining. It is not commonly found in food sources but may be present in trace amounts in some soils.

- **Caesium**: A trace element found in small amounts in various foods, caesium is thought to support the nervous system but is not essential to human health.

- **Tellurium**: This trace element is involved in antioxidant defence and is found in mushrooms and garlic.

Analogy: Minerals as Cogs in a Well-Oiled Machine

Minerals are like the individual cogs in a well-oiled machine—each one plays a specific and essential role in keeping the system running smoothly. Just as the failure of one cog can lead to the breakdown of the entire machine, a deficiency in one mineral can disrupt numerous physiological processes. Calcium, magnesium, and potassium are like the large cogs that drive the main gears of muscle function, bone health, and fluid balance. Meanwhile, trace elements like selenium and iodine are smaller, more specialised cogs that fine-tune the machine, ensuring everything operates at peak efficiency. Without them, the entire system may falter, leading to a cascade of health problems.

Summary: Understanding the Essential Minerals – Their Functions and Natural Sources

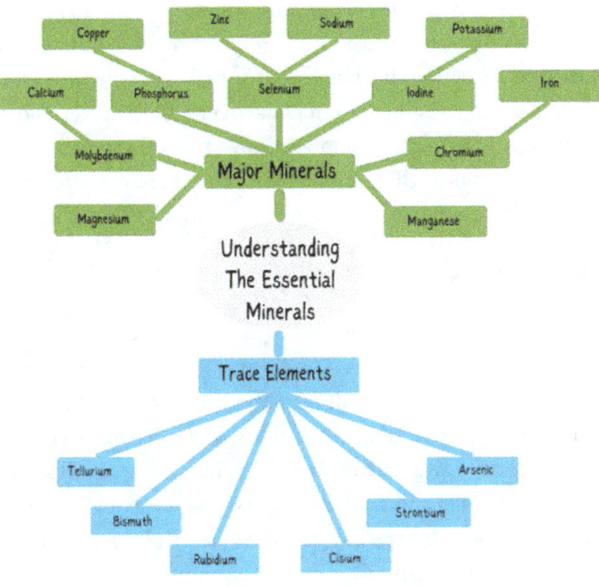

Chapter 4
Celtic Salt – A Natural Source of Trace Minerals

Celtic salt is a powerful and ancient source of vital minerals that have been used for centuries to support human health. Unlike modern refined table salt, which is stripped of its natural minerals during processing, Celtic salt retains over 80 minerals and trace elements essential for various bodily functions. This chapter explores the origins of Celtic salt, the minerals it contains, its health benefits, and how it compares to refined table salt.

What is Celtic Salt?

Celtic salt, also known as sel gris (grey salt), is harvested traditionally from the coastal regions of Brittany, France. The process of collecting Celtic salt is a time-honoured practice that has been passed down through generations of salt farmers. The salt is harvested from seawater that naturally flows into shallow pools, where it evaporates under the sun. As the water evaporates, salt crystals form and are carefully raked by hand using wooden tools, ensuring that the natural mineral content is preserved. The traditional methods used in its production mean that it remains unrefined, unlike commercial table salt.

What sets Celtic salt apart from other salts is its distinctive grey colour, which comes from the mineral-rich clay in the salt flats where it is harvested. The clay contributes additional trace elements, further enhancing the nutritional value of the salt. Celtic salt's moisture content is also higher than that of regular table salt, giving it a moist texture and a more complex flavour profile.

Minerals Found in Celtic Salt

Celtic salt contains a wide variety of essential minerals and trace elements, making it one of the most mineral-rich salts available. Here are some of the essential minerals found in Celtic salt:

- **Sodium and Chloride:** These are the primary components of salt, essential for maintaining fluid balance, nerve transmission, and muscle function.

- **Magnesium:** Supports muscle relaxation, nerve function, and bone health.

- **Potassium:** Helps regulate fluid balance, muscle contractions, and nerve signals.

- **Calcium:** Essential for strong bones and teeth, as well as muscle function and nerve signalling.

- **Iron:** Important for oxygen transport in the blood and energy production.

- **Zinc:** Plays a role in immune function, wound healing, and DNA synthesis.

- **Copper:** Supports iron metabolism, connective tissue formation, and brain function.

- **Manganese:** Involved in bone formation, metabolism, and antioxidant defence.

- **Selenium:** A powerful antioxidant that supports thyroid function and immune health.

- **Fluoride:** Strengthens teeth and bones.

- **Iodine:** Crucial for thyroid hormone production and metabolic regulation.

- **Silicon**: Supports connective tissue health and skin elasticity.

- **Sulfur**: A key component of amino acids and involved in detoxification processes.

- **Boron**: Supports bone health and hormone regulation.

- **Strontium**: Promotes bone strength and mimics calcium in the body.

- **Nickel**: Involved in enzymatic processes.

- **Vanadium**: Supports cardiovascular health and blood sugar regulation.

- **Lithium**: May have mood-stabilising effects and supports brain function.

- **Germanium**: Has antioxidant properties and may enhance the immune system.

- **Rubidium**: Plays a role in maintaining cellular energy and electrolyte balance.

These are just a few of the minerals found in Celtic salt, but it contains over 80 trace elements that contribute to its overall health benefits. Unlike refined table salt, which only contains sodium chloride, Celtic salt offers a wide spectrum of minerals that are essential for the body's optimal function.

Health Benefits of Celtic Salt

Celtic salt's rich mineral content offers numerous health benefits, particularly for those looking to balance their electrolyte levels, support bone health, enhance muscle function, and improve overall metabolic health. Let's take a closer look at some of the specific health benefits:

1. **Electrolyte Balance**: Electrolytes are minerals that help regulate fluid balance, muscle contractions, and nerve function. Sodium, chloride, potassium, magnesium, and calcium—five of the most important electrolytes—are all present in Celtic salt. This makes it an excellent natural option for replenishing electrolytes lost through sweat, particularly during exercise or in hot climates. Many athletes and individuals with physically demanding lifestyles find that switching to Celtic salt improves their hydration and muscle recovery.

2. **Bone Health**: The calcium, magnesium, and phosphorus found in Celtic salt play a vital role in maintaining strong bones and teeth. These minerals help to regulate bone density and prevent conditions like osteoporosis. The trace elements, such as strontium and boron, further support bone health by enhancing the body's ability to retain calcium and promoting the formation of new bone tissue.

3. **Muscle Function**: Magnesium and potassium are essential for proper muscle function, including contraction and relaxation. A deficiency in either of these minerals can lead to muscle cramps, spasms, and weakness. Celtic salt provides these minerals in a natural form, making it a valuable tool for preventing muscle cramps and improving muscle endurance.

4. **Metabolic Health**: Iodine, zinc, and selenium—three minerals present in Celtic salt—are critical for supporting thyroid health and regulating metabolism. Iodine helps the thyroid gland produce hormones that control metabolic processes, while selenium acts as an antioxidant that protects the thyroid from oxidative damage. Zinc supports the production of thyroid hormones and helps maintain a healthy immune system.

5. **Detoxification**: The sulfur and silicon in Celtic salt support the body's detoxification processes. Sulfur is a key component of amino acids involved in detox pathways, helping the liver break down toxins. Silicon contributes to connective tissue

health and assists in the removal of waste products from the body.

6. **Cardiovascular Health**: Potassium and magnesium help regulate blood pressure by balancing sodium levels in the body. While excessive sodium can contribute to high blood pressure, the presence of potassium and magnesium in Celtic salt helps counterbalance this effect, promoting cardiovascular health.

Comparison to Table Salt

The contrast between Celtic salt and refined table salt is stark, particularly in terms of their mineral content and health implications. Refined table salt is almost entirely sodium chloride, with additives like anti-caking agents to prevent clumping. During the refining process, table salt is stripped of its natural minerals, leaving behind only sodium chloride. In some cases, table salt is fortified with iodine, but it lacks the full spectrum of trace minerals found in unrefined salts like Celtic salt.

Consuming excessive amounts of refined table salt, which lacks potassium and magnesium, can contribute to electrolyte imbalances, leading to high blood pressure, fluid retention, and other health issues. Additionally, the absence of trace elements in refined salt means that it offers no additional nutritional benefits beyond sodium chloride, which can strain the body's ability to maintain mineral balance.

On the other hand, Celtic salt, with its natural composition of over 80 trace elements, provides a balanced source of electrolytes and other minerals. It supports hydration, bone health, and muscle function, making it a far superior option for maintaining health.

Case History: Muscle Cramps and Fatigue

Consider the case of a 45-year-old woman who frequently experienced muscle cramps and fatigue, especially after exercise. Despite staying hydrated and eating a balanced diet, her symptoms persisted. After discussing her mineral intake with a nutritionist, she learned that her body may be lacking in key electrolytes like magnesium and potassium. At the nutritionist's recommendation, she began using Celtic salt in her meals and as a mineral supplement during workouts.

Within weeks of making the switch, she noticed a significant reduction in muscle cramps and an improvement in her energy levels. The added magnesium and potassium from Celtic salt helped restore her electrolyte balance, while the trace elements supported overall metabolic function. Her experience illustrates the profound impact that a simple dietary change—incorporating mineral-rich Celtic salt—can have on improving muscle function and reducing fatigue.

Conclusion

Celtic salt stands out as a natural, unrefined source of essential minerals that support a wide range of bodily functions. Its rich mineral content, including over 80 trace elements, makes it an excellent alternative to refined table salt. It lacks the diversity of nutrients needed to maintain electrolyte balance, muscle function, bone health, and metabolic stability. By integrating Celtic salt into the diet, individuals can enjoy its many health benefits, particularly in maintaining proper mineral balance in today's modern, mineral-depleted food environment. Whether used for cooking, seasoning, or electrolyte replenishment, Celtic salt offers a simple yet powerful way to enhance health naturally.

Summary:Celtic Salt – A Natural Source of Trace Minerals

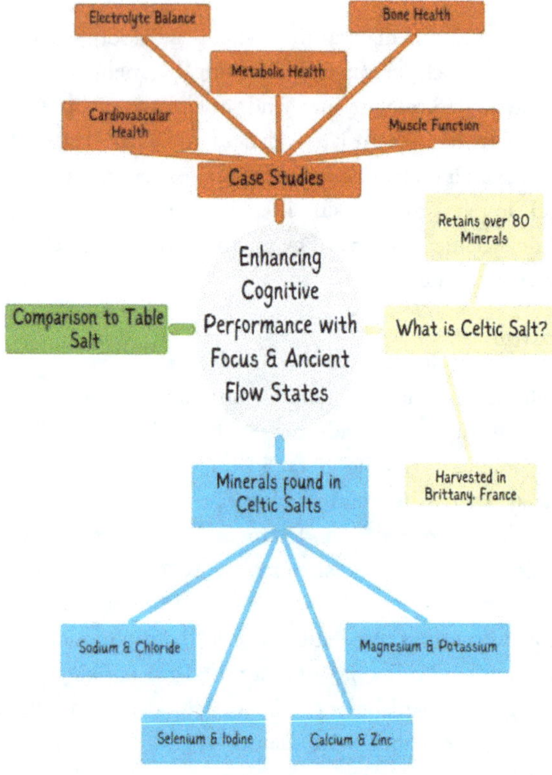

Chapter 5
The Science of Mineral Absorption – How It Works

Minerals play an essential role in human health, but their benefits are only realised when they are absorbed and utilised by the body. The process of mineral absorption is complex and involves multiple organs and biochemical processes. Understanding how minerals are absorbed, the factors that affect this absorption, and how vitamins play a crucial role in enhancing it is key to ensuring that our bodies receive the nutrients they need. This chapter delves into the mechanisms of mineral absorption, explores the factors that can influence how well minerals are absorbed, and provides insights into improving bioavailability.

How Minerals Are Absorbed

Minerals are absorbed in the digestive tract, primarily in the small intestine. However, the process starts in the stomach, where digestive enzymes and stomach acid begin breaking down food, releasing minerals for absorption.

The Stomach's Role

The stomach produces hydrochloric acid (HCl), which helps break down food into smaller particles, making it easier for the body to extract minerals. Stomach acid is particularly important for the absorption of minerals like calcium, magnesium, and iron. In acidic conditions, these minerals become ionised, making them easier to absorb. Without sufficient stomach acid, the body struggles to extract and absorb certain minerals, which is why conditions like hypochlorhydria (low stomach acid) can lead to deficiencies in key minerals.

The Small Intestine's Role

After food leaves the stomach, it enters the small intestine, where most mineral absorption takes place. The small intestine is lined with specialised cells called enterocytes, which are responsible for transporting minerals from the digestive tract into the bloodstream. Each mineral has its own specific transport mechanism. For example, calcium is absorbed through both passive diffusion and active transport, which is regulated by the body's calcium levels and vitamin D.

Enzymes and transporter proteins in the small intestine play a vital role in ensuring that minerals are absorbed efficiently. These enzymes break down food into its component nutrients, making minerals available for absorption. Transporter proteins then carry minerals across the intestinal wall and into the bloodstream, where they are distributed throughout the body to be used in various physiological processes.

The Large Intestine's Role

While the small intestine absorbs the majority of minerals, the large intestine (colon) can also absorb certain minerals, particularly electrolytes like sodium, potassium, and chloride. This secondary absorption process is essential for maintaining fluid balance and preventing dehydration.

Factors Affecting Mineral Absorption

Several factors influence how well the body absorbs minerals. These factors include gut health, interactions between minerals, and the presence of vitamins that facilitate mineral absorption.

Gut Health and Mineral Absorption

A healthy gut is crucial for proper mineral absorption. The integrity of the gut lining, the balance of gut bacteria (microbiota), and the overall health of the digestive system all play significant roles in how efficiently minerals are absorbed.

- **Gut Lining**: The gut lining acts as a barrier that controls what enters the bloodstream. If the lining is damaged, as in the case of conditions like leaky gut syndrome, the absorption of minerals can be impaired. Chronic inflammation of the gut, such as in inflammatory bowel disease (IBD), can also reduce the ability of the intestines to absorb minerals effectively, leading to deficiencies.

- **Gut Microbiota**: The gut microbiota, the community of bacteria that reside in the digestive tract, play a role in breaking down food and aiding in the absorption of certain minerals. For example, some bacteria in the gut can help release minerals like magnesium and calcium from food. An imbalance in gut bacteria (dysbiosis) can interfere with this process, leading to suboptimal absorption of essential minerals.

- **Digestive Enzymes**: The pancreas produces enzymes that help break down food in the small intestine, making minerals available for absorption. If enzyme production is compromised, as in the case of pancreatic insufficiency, the body may struggle to absorb minerals effectively.

Competing Minerals: How Interactions Affect Absorption

One of the most important factors affecting mineral absorption is the interaction between different minerals. Certain minerals can compete with one another for absorption, which means that high intakes of one mineral can inhibit the absorption of another.

- **Calcium and Magnesium**: Calcium and magnesium are both essential minerals, but they can compete for absorption in the small intestine. Large doses of calcium can reduce magnesium absorption and vice versa. This competition occurs because they use similar transport mechanisms to cross the intestinal lining. For individuals who take supplements for both minerals, it's often recommended to space out their intake to avoid this competition.

- **Zinc and Iron**: Zinc and iron are another pair of minerals that can compete for absorption. Both minerals use the same transporter proteins to be absorbed, so high intakes of one mineral can inhibit the absorption of the other. This is particularly important for individuals who rely on supplements, as taking high doses of zinc, for example, can lead to lower iron absorption and potentially cause iron deficiency anaemia over time.

- **Calcium and Iron**: Calcium can interfere with the absorption of non-heme iron (the form of iron found in plant-based foods). This is why it's often recommended to avoid consuming calcium-rich foods or supplements at the same time as iron-rich meals or supplements.

These interactions highlight the importance of balanced mineral intake and paying attention to how different minerals are consumed in relation to one another.

The Role of Vitamins in Mineral Absorption

Vitamins often work hand-in-hand with minerals, enhancing their absorption and ensuring that they are effectively utilised by the body. Two key vitamins that play a crucial role in mineral absorption are vitamin D and vitamin C.

Vitamin D and Calcium Absorption

Vitamin D is essential for the absorption of calcium. Without sufficient vitamin D, the body cannot absorb calcium effectively, even if dietary calcium intake is adequate. Vitamin D helps regulate the production of calcium-binding proteins in the intestines, which transport calcium into the bloodstream.

People with vitamin D deficiency often experience poor calcium absorption, leading to weakened bones and an increased risk of conditions like osteoporosis. This is why vitamin D supplementation is often recommended for individuals with low bone density, as it ensures that the calcium consumed through diet or supplements is properly absorbed.

Vitamin C and Iron Absorption

Vitamin C is critical for enhancing the absorption of non-heme iron, the type of iron found in plant-based foods. Non-heme iron is less readily absorbed by the body compared to heme iron (found in animal products), but vitamin C can significantly boost its absorption. It does this by reducing ferric iron (Fe^{3+}) to ferrous iron (Fe^{2+}), a form that is more easily absorbed by the intestines.

For vegetarians, vegans, or individuals with low iron levels, consuming vitamin C-rich foods like citrus fruits, bell peppers, or strawberries alongside iron-rich plant foods can improve iron absorption and reduce the risk of iron deficiency anaemia.

Bioavailability: The Forms of Minerals Matter

Not all forms of minerals are created equal when it comes to absorption. The bioavailability of a mineral refers to how easily it can be absorbed and utilised by the body. Some forms of minerals are more bioavailable than others, meaning that they are absorbed more efficiently and are more likely to produce the desired health benefits.

Magnesium: Oxide vs. Glycinate

Magnesium is available in several different forms, and the bioavailability of each form can vary significantly.

- **Magnesium Oxide**: This form of magnesium is commonly found in supplements, but it has relatively low bioavailability. Studies have shown that only about 4% of magnesium from magnesium oxide is absorbed by the body. Despite its low absorption rate, it is often used in supplements because it is inexpensive and easy to manufacture.

- **Magnesium Glycinate**: Magnesium glycinate is a chelated form of magnesium, meaning it is bound to the amino acid glycine. This form of magnesium has much higher bioavailability, as the body absorbs it more easily. Magnesium glycinate is often recommended for individuals with magnesium deficiencies, as it is less likely to cause digestive upset and provides a more reliable source of magnesium for the body.

Calcium: Carbonate vs. Citrate

Calcium is another mineral that comes in different forms, each with varying levels of bioavailability.

- **Calcium Carbonate**: This is the most common form of calcium found in supplements. It contains a high percentage of elemental calcium, but it requires sufficient stomach acid for absorption. Individuals with low stomach acid or digestive issues may struggle to absorb calcium carbonate efficiently.

- **Calcium Citrate**: Calcium citrate is more easily absorbed than calcium carbonate and does not require stomach acid for absorption. This makes it a better option for individuals with lower stomach acid levels, such as older adults or those taking acid-reducing medications.

Case History: Gut Health and Iron Absorption

Consider the case of a 32-year-old woman who struggled with chronic fatigue and low energy levels. Blood tests revealed that she had low iron levels despite taking iron supplements regularly. Her doctor also diagnosed her with gut inflammation, specifically related to a condition called small intestinal bacterial overgrowth (SIBO), which was contributing to malabsorption issues.

After addressing the underlying gut inflammation through a gut healing protocol that included probiotics, anti-inflammatory foods, and the removal of irritants, her iron levels began to improve. By healing her gut, she was able to absorb iron more effectively, leading to better energy levels and a resolution of her chronic fatigue. This case highlights the importance of gut health in mineral absorption and demonstrates that simply taking supplements may not be enough if the digestive system is not functioning properly.

Conclusion

The science of mineral absorption is a complex but essential aspect of human nutrition. From the stomach's role in breaking down food and releasing minerals to the small intestine's transport mechanisms and the factors that influence absorption, it's clear that ensuring optimal mineral intake requires more than just consuming mineral-rich foods. Gut health, competing minerals, and the presence of vitamins like vitamin D and vitamin C are all critical in determining how well the body absorbs and utilises minerals. Understanding the bioavailability of different mineral forms is also essential for choosing the right supplements to meet individual needs.

By focusing on the science of absorption and addressing factors like gut health and nutrient interactions, we can optimise our mineral intake and ensure that the body receives the vital nutrients it needs for optimal health and function.

Summary:The Science of Mineral Absorption – How It Works

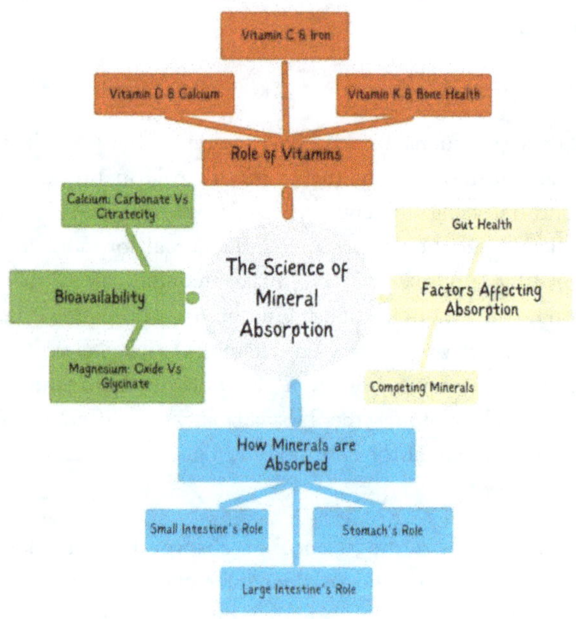

Chapter 6
Oral Supplementation –
Best Practices and Dosages

Minerals are essential for optimal health, but modern diets often fall short of providing adequate levels of these nutrients. Oral supplementation offers a practical way to address mineral deficiencies, but with so many options available—capsules, powders, chelated forms, and liquid minerals—choosing the right supplement can be confusing. In this chapter, we'll explore the different types of mineral supplements, how to select the right one based on individual needs, dosage recommendations, safety considerations, and real-life examples of how proper supplementation can dramatically improve health.

Different Types of Supplements

When it comes to mineral supplements, there are several forms to choose from, each with its own advantages and considerations. Understanding the differences between these forms is key to selecting the best option for your health needs.

Capsules

Capsules are among the most common and convenient forms of mineral supplements. They are easy to swallow, widely available, and come in various dosages. Capsules typically contain mineral salts or chelated minerals, which are bound to amino acids to enhance absorption. The capsule dissolves in the stomach, releasing the minerals for absorption in the intestines.

- **Advantages**: Capsules are easy to take, store, and transport. They are often available in standardised doses, making it simple to track intake.

- **Considerations**: Some people may have difficulty swallowing capsules, and the absorption rate can vary depending on the form of the mineral used.

Powders

Mineral powders are another popular form of supplementation. They can be mixed into water, smoothies, or other beverages, making them a versatile option for individuals who prefer not to take capsules.

- **Advantages**: Powders offer flexibility in dosage, allowing users to adjust their intake according to their needs. They are also absorbed more quickly than capsules, as they do not need to dissolve in the stomach.

- **Considerations**: The taste of mineral powders can be unpleasant for some people, and careful measuring is required to ensure proper dosing.

Chelated Forms

Chelated minerals are minerals that are bound to organic compounds, usually amino acids, to enhance their absorption in the digestive tract. Common examples include magnesium glycinate and zinc picolinate. Chelated forms are often preferred for their superior bioavailability, meaning they are absorbed more effectively by the body compared to non-chelated forms.

- **Advantages**: Chelated minerals are generally easier to absorb, reducing the risk of gastrointestinal discomfort. They are particularly beneficial for people with digestive issues or poor nutrient absorption.

- **Considerations**: Chelated supplements tend to be more expensive than other forms and may not be necessary for individuals with normal digestive function.

Liquid Minerals

Liquid mineral supplements offer a highly absorbable option, as they bypass the digestive process to some extent. Liquid forms are ideal for people who have trouble swallowing capsules or for those with compromised digestive systems.

- **Advantages**: Liquid minerals are quickly absorbed and can be easily added to beverages. They are also easier to dose for individuals who need smaller or more precise amounts of minerals.

- **Considerations**: Liquid supplements may not have as long of a shelf life as capsules or powders and often require refrigeration. Some individuals may find the taste unappealing.

How to Choose the Right Supplement

Selecting the right mineral supplement depends on a variety of factors, including your dietary habits, lifestyle, health status, and specific mineral deficiencies. Here are some considerations for choosing the best supplement for your needs:

Assessing Individual Needs

The first step in selecting the right mineral supplement is understanding your specific nutritional needs. Some individuals may require higher doses of certain minerals due to age, medical conditions, or lifestyle factors. For example, athletes may need more magnesium and potassium to support muscle function and electrolyte balance, while postmenopausal women may require more calcium to maintain bone health.

- **Diet**: If your diet lacks mineral-rich foods such as leafy greens, nuts, seeds, and whole grains, you may need a broader spectrum mineral supplement. Conversely, if you already consume a mineral-rich diet, you might only need to supplement with specific minerals.

- **Health Conditions**: Certain health conditions, such as osteoporosis, anaemia, or high blood pressure, may increase your need for specific minerals like calcium, iron, or magnesium. In these cases, targeted supplementation is necessary to address deficiencies.

- **Lifestyle**: Individuals who engage in strenuous physical activity, experience high levels of stress, or live in environments with depleted soils may have higher mineral needs. For example, athletes may benefit from additional magnesium and potassium to prevent muscle cramps and maintain electrolyte balance.

Testing for Deficiencies

Testing your mineral levels through blood or hair analysis can provide valuable insights into which minerals you may be deficient in. This is especially useful for minerals like magnesium, iron, and zinc, where deficiencies can cause specific symptoms but may not be immediately obvious without testing.

- **Magnesium Deficiency**: Symptoms of magnesium deficiency include muscle cramps, fatigue, irritability, and irregular heartbeats. A blood test can confirm low magnesium levels, and supplementation can be tailored accordingly.

- **Iron Deficiency**: Common signs of iron deficiency include fatigue, pale skin, and shortness of breath. Blood tests, such as serum ferritin levels, can diagnose iron deficiency, particularly in individuals with anaemia.

- **Zinc Deficiency**: Low zinc levels can manifest as a weakened immune system, slow wound healing, and hair loss. Zinc supplementation can help restore optimal levels, but it is important to test for deficiencies before starting supplementation.

Dosage Recommendations

Once you've identified which minerals you need to supplement, it's important to follow appropriate dosage guidelines to avoid deficiencies or overdoses. Here are the recommended daily dosages for key minerals:

Calcium

- **Recommended Daily Intake**: 1,000 mg/day for adults, increasing to 1,200 mg/day for women over 50 and men over 70.

- **When Higher Doses Are Needed**: Individuals with osteoporosis, postmenopausal women, and those on certain medications may need higher doses. Always consult a healthcare provider before taking high doses of calcium.

Magnesium

- **Recommended Daily Intake**: 400-420 mg/day for men, 310-320 mg/day for women.

- **When Higher Doses Are Needed**: Athletes, individuals with high-stress levels, and those with digestive disorders may require more magnesium. Chelated forms like magnesium glycinate or magnesium malate are often recommended for better absorption.

Iron

- **Recommended Daily Intake**: 8 mg/day for men, 18 mg/day for women of childbearing age. Pregnant women need 27 mg/day.

- **When Higher Doses Are Needed**: People with iron deficiency anaemia or those with heavy menstrual periods may require higher doses. Supplementation should be done under medical supervision, as excessive iron can be harmful.

Potassium

- **Recommended Daily Intake**: 2,500-3,000 mg/day for adults.

- **When Higher Doses Are Needed**: Potassium supplementation is generally not recommended unless prescribed by a healthcare provider. People with low potassium levels due to diuretic use or excessive sweating may need to increase their intake.

Zinc

- **Recommended Daily Intake**: 8-11 mg/day for adults.

- **When Higher Doses Are Needed**: Higher doses may be recommended for individuals with immune deficiencies, slow wound healing, or certain medical conditions. Zinc supplementation should not exceed 40 mg/day, as excessive intake can lead to imbalances with copper.

Selenium

- **Recommended Daily Intake**: 55 mcg/day for adults.

- **When Higher Doses Are Needed**: Selenium deficiency is rare, but higher doses may be required in areas with selenium-deficient soils. Excessive selenium intake can be toxic, so it's important not to exceed 400 mcg/day.

Safety Considerations

While mineral supplementation can be beneficial for addressing deficiencies, it's important to approach supplementation with caution, especially for minerals that can be toxic at high doses. Overdosing on minerals like iron, zinc, and selenium can cause serious health problems, including toxicity and interference with the absorption of other minerals.

Iron Overdose

Iron is essential for oxygen transport, but too much iron can lead to iron overload, a condition that damages organs like the liver and heart. Hemochromatosis, a genetic disorder that causes the body to store too much iron, is a major risk for individuals who take high doses of iron supplements without medical supervision. Symptoms of iron toxicity include nausea, vomiting, abdominal pain, and, in severe cases, organ failure.

Zinc Imbalance

While zinc is important for immune function and wound healing, excessive zinc intake can interfere with the absorption of other essential minerals, particularly copper. High doses of zinc (over 40 mg/day) for extended periods can lead to a copper deficiency, resulting in anaemia and neurological issues. It's important to balance zinc supplementation with adequate copper intake, especially in long-term use.

Selenium Toxicity

Selenium is a powerful antioxidant, but excessive intake can lead to selenium toxicity, a condition known as selenosis. Symptoms include gastrointestinal distress, hair loss, fatigue, and, in severe cases, neurological damage. The tolerable upper intake level for selenium is 400 mcg/day, and it's crucial to avoid exceeding this limit.

General Safety Tips

- **Consult with a Healthcare Provider**: Before starting any mineral supplementation, especially in high doses, it's important to consult with a healthcare provider to ensure that supplementation is appropriate for your needs and won't interfere with other medications or conditions.

- **Follow Dosage Guidelines**: Always follow the recommended dosage on supplement labels and avoid self-prescribing high doses of minerals without medical advice.

- **Consider Form and Absorption**: Choosing the right form of a mineral (e.g., chelated vs. non-chelated) can make a significant difference in how well your body absorbs it. Pay attention to bioavailability when selecting a supplement.

Case History: Balancing Sodium, Potassium, and Magnesium for Cardiovascular Health

John, a 50-year-old man, came to his doctor complaining of fatigue, muscle cramps, and high blood pressure. His lifestyle included a high-stress job and frequent business travel, which left little time for exercise or healthy meals. After a blood test, his doctor found that John's sodium levels were elevated, while his potassium and magnesium levels were lower than optimal.

John's doctor recommended a comprehensive mineral supplementation plan, focusing on reducing sodium intake and increasing his potassium and magnesium levels. He started taking a magnesium glycinate supplement and included more potassium-rich foods like bananas, sweet potatoes, and leafy greens in his diet. In addition, John cut back on processed foods high in sodium and replaced them with fresh, whole foods.

Within three months, John saw significant improvements in his cardiovascular health. His blood pressure normalised, his muscle cramps disappeared, and his energy levels increased. By balancing his mineral intake, John was able to improve his overall well-being and reduce his reliance on medications for blood pressure management.

Conclusion

Oral supplementation offers a practical and effective way to address mineral deficiencies, but choosing the right supplement and dosage is essential for optimal results. Whether you opt for capsules, powders, chelated forms, or liquid minerals, it's important to consider your individual needs, health conditions, and lifestyle when selecting a supplement. Monitoring your intake, ensuring balanced levels, and consulting with healthcare professionals can help you safely and effectively improve your mineral status for long-term health and well-being.

Summary:Oral Supplementation – Best Practices and Dosages

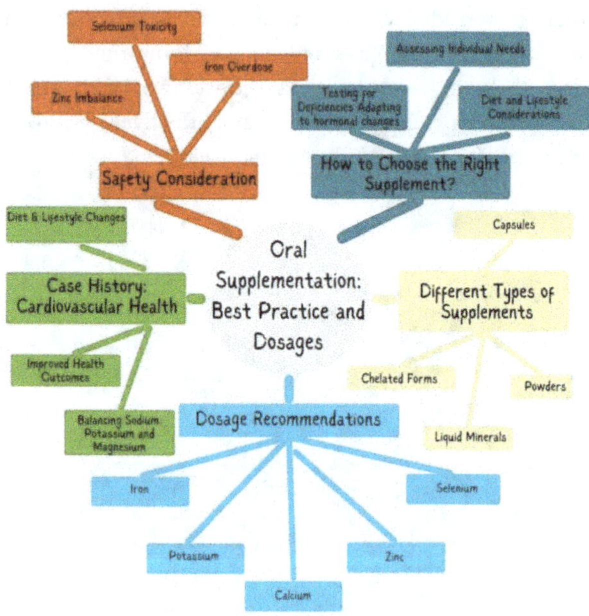

Chapter 7
The Case for IV Mineral Therapy

Intravenous (IV) mineral therapy has gained popularity as a potent and efficient method for delivering essential minerals directly into the bloodstream. By bypassing the digestive system, IV therapy ensures immediate absorption and utilisation of nutrients, making it an attractive option for people who need rapid replenishment of minerals. In this chapter, we will explore the science behind IV mineral therapy, who benefits most from this treatment, the types of IV drips available, and the advantages of IV therapy over oral supplementation. A real-life case history will also illustrate how IV mineral therapy can enhance performance and recovery in athletes.

What is IV Mineral Therapy?

IV mineral therapy involves the direct administration of minerals into the bloodstream through an intravenous drip. Unlike oral supplements, which must pass through the digestive system before being absorbed, IV therapy allows for 100% bioavailability of minerals. This means the body can use these minerals immediately, making IV therapy a powerful option for individuals who have difficulty absorbing minerals or who need quick and efficient replenishment.

The process of IV mineral therapy is straightforward. A healthcare provider inserts an IV catheter into a vein, usually in the arm, and the mineral solution is delivered slowly over a period of 30 minutes to several hours, depending on the type and volume of minerals being administered. The patient remains comfortable during the process, and because the minerals are delivered directly into the bloodstream, they are distributed throughout the body without delay.

IV mineral therapy is often administered in medical clinics or wellness centres, under the supervision of healthcare professionals. It is used not only to treat specific mineral deficiencies but also as part of wellness programs designed to optimise health, reduce fatigue, and improve physical and cognitive performance.

Who Benefits the Most from IV Mineral Therapy?

IV mineral therapy can benefit a wide range of individuals, but it is particularly effective for those with specific conditions or needs. Here are the groups that typically benefit the most:

1. People with Severe Mineral Deficiencies

Some individuals suffer from severe mineral deficiencies that cannot be corrected through diet or oral supplements alone. This can occur due to medical conditions such as malnutrition, chronic illness, or after surgery. For example, people with iron deficiency anaemia may not respond well to oral iron supplements due to poor absorption or digestive side effects, making IV iron therapy a preferred treatment option.

2. Individuals with Gut Absorption Issues

Gut health plays a crucial role in mineral absorption, and individuals with conditions like Crohn's disease, ulcerative colitis, celiac disease, or leaky gut syndrome may struggle to absorb minerals through the digestive tract. In these cases, IV therapy offers a way to bypass the gut and deliver essential nutrients directly into the bloodstream, ensuring that deficiencies are corrected efficiently.

Patients who have undergone gastrointestinal surgery or those with conditions like irritable bowel syndrome (IBS) or small intestinal bacterial overgrowth (SIBO) may also benefit from IV mineral therapy, as their ability to absorb minerals from food and supplements is often compromised.

3. Those Needing Rapid Replenishment

Certain situations require the rapid replenishment of minerals. Athletes, for example, may need to restore electrolyte levels quickly after intense training or competition to enhance recovery and performance. Similarly, people suffering from acute dehydration, prolonged illness, or chronic fatigue may benefit from the quick-acting effects of IV mineral therapy.

Individuals recovering from surgery, chemotherapy, or other medical treatments that deplete the body's mineral stores may also require rapid replenishment to aid in recovery and healing. In these cases, IV mineral therapy can provide an immediate boost of nutrients that oral supplementation cannot match.

4. People with High-Stress Lifestyles

Chronic stress depletes the body's mineral stores, particularly magnesium and potassium, which are essential for managing stress and supporting nervous system function for individuals who experience high levels of stress, whether due to a demanding job, personal life pressures, or ongoing mental health issues, IV mineral therapy offers a way to quickly restore depleted minerals and improve stress resilience.

5. Individuals Seeking Overall Wellness

IV mineral therapy is not just for those with deficiencies or medical conditions. Many people use it as part of a wellness routine to enhance their energy levels, support immune function, and improve overall health. Multi-mineral drips, which contain a combination of essential minerals like magnesium, calcium, zinc, and selenium, can help optimise physical and cognitive performance, reduce fatigue, and promote long-term wellness.

Types of IV Mineral Drips

There are different types of IV mineral drips available, each designed to address specific health concerns or wellness goals. Some of the most common types include:

1. Magnesium Drips for Stress Relief

Magnesium is a vital mineral involved in over 300 enzymatic reactions in the body, including those related to muscle function, energy production, and nervous system health. Magnesium deficiency is widespread, especially among individuals under chronic stress or those with poor dietary intake. IV magnesium drips are commonly used to alleviate symptoms of magnesium deficiency, including muscle cramps, fatigue, and stress-related disorders.

Magnesium drips work by relaxing muscles and calming the nervous system, making them an effective treatment for individuals experiencing high levels of anxiety or those with conditions like migraines or tension headaches. The quick absorption of magnesium through IV therapy ensures rapid relief from symptoms, and many individuals report feeling calmer and more energised after treatment.

2. Multi-Mineral Drips for Overall Wellness

Multi-mineral drips contain a blend of essential minerals, including magnesium, calcium, potassium, zinc, and selenium, among others. These drips are designed to support overall health and wellness by replenishing depleted mineral stores and improving the body's ability to function optimally.

Multi-mineral drips are often used by individuals looking to boost their immune system, enhance cognitive function, and improve energy levels. They are also popular among athletes and people recovering from illness, as the combination of minerals helps the body repair tissues, maintain electrolyte balance, and support recovery.

3. Potassium Drips for Electrolyte Balance

Potassium is an essential electrolyte that plays a key role in regulating fluid balance, muscle contractions, and nerve function. Potassium deficiencies can occur due to dehydration, excessive sweating, or certain medications like diuretics. IV potassium drips are commonly used to restore electrolyte balance in individuals who are dehydrated, experiencing muscle cramps, or suffering from low potassium levels (hypokalemia).

By administering potassium directly into the bloodstream, IV therapy ensures that electrolyte levels are restored quickly and effectively, preventing complications like arrhythmias, muscle weakness, and fatigue.

Advantages Over Oral Supplements

While oral supplements are effective for maintaining adequate mineral levels in many people, IV mineral therapy offers several distinct advantages, particularly for individuals with specific health needs:

1. Immediate Absorption

One of the primary advantages of IV mineral therapy is its immediate absorption. Since minerals are delivered directly into the bloodstream, they bypass the digestive system entirely. This ensures 100% bioavailability, meaning the body can use the minerals immediately without the delay or loss that can occur with oral supplementation. This is particularly beneficial for individuals with digestive issues that impair nutrient absorption.

2. No Loss Through Digestion

Oral supplements must pass through the digestive system, where various factors can affect their absorption. For example, some minerals, like magnesium and calcium, compete for absorption in the intestines, reducing their bioavailability. Similarly, conditions like low stomach acid, leaky gut, or inflammatory bowel disease can interfere with the body's ability to absorb minerals from supplements.

IV therapy eliminates these issues by delivering minerals directly into the bloodstream, where they can be used by the body without any loss through digestion. This makes IV therapy a more efficient and effective method for correcting deficiencies and restoring optimal mineral levels.

3. Customisation and Personalisation

IV mineral therapy allows for precise customisation based on an individual's specific needs. A healthcare provider can tailor the mineral drip to address deficiencies or health concerns unique to each person, ensuring that they receive the exact minerals and dosages needed for optimal results. This level of personalisation is often not possible with standard oral supplements, which come in fixed doses and formulations.

4. Rapid Replenishment

For individuals needing quick relief from symptoms or rapid replenishment of depleted mineral stores, IV therapy provides a fast and effective solution. Oral supplements can take days or even weeks to build up mineral levels in the body, while IV therapy delivers immediate results. This is especially beneficial for athletes, individuals recovering from illness, or those experiencing acute mineral deficiencies.

Case History: An Athlete's Experience with IV Magnesium and Potassium Drips

Sarah, a 28-year-old professional triathlete, was experiencing muscle cramps, fatigue, and slow recovery times after training sessions. Despite eating a balanced diet and taking oral supplements, she struggled to maintain adequate electrolyte levels, particularly magnesium and potassium, due to the intense physical demands of her training regimen.

After consulting with a sports nutritionist, Sarah decided to try IV mineral therapy. She received a series of magnesium and potassium drips designed to replenish her electrolyte levels and support muscle recovery. The results were immediate—her muscle cramps disappeared, and she felt more energised during her workouts. Additionally, her recovery times improved, allowing her to train more effectively without experiencing the same level of fatigue or muscle soreness.

Sarah continued to use IV mineral therapy as part of her training routine, receiving drips every few weeks to maintain optimal mineral levels. By incorporating IV therapy into her regimen, she was able to enhance her performance, prevent dehydration, and improve her overall recovery and endurance.

Conclusion

IV mineral therapy offers a powerful and efficient way to restore and maintain optimal mineral levels, particularly for individuals with severe deficiencies, gut absorption issues, or those who need rapid replenishment. With its immediate absorption and customisable formulations, IV therapy provides a unique advantage over oral supplements, ensuring that the body receives the minerals it needs without delay or digestive interference.

Whether used to correct deficiencies, support athletic performance, or promote overall wellness, IV mineral therapy is a valuable tool in modern health and nutrition. By delivering essential minerals directly into the bloodstream, this therapy offers a faster, more effective solution for replenishing depleted nutrients and supporting long-term health and vitality.

Summary: The Case for IV Mineral Therapy

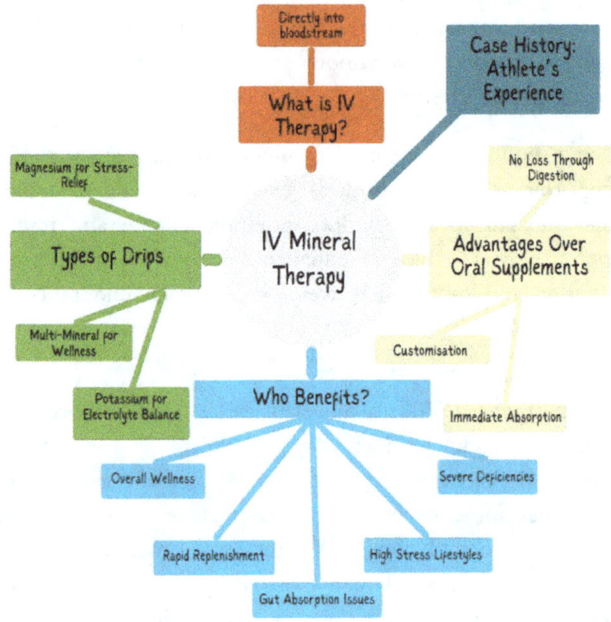

Chapter 8
Case Histories – The Miracles of Mineral Replenishment

Minerals are the building blocks of human health, playing crucial roles in everything from energy production to immune function, bone health, and mental well-being. While modern diets often fall short of providing the necessary levels of these essential nutrients, supplementation can make a significant difference in correcting deficiencies and restoring health. In this chapter, we explore four powerful case histories that illustrate the transformative effects of mineral replenishment.

Story 1: Reversing Chronic Fatigue with Magnesium and Iron Supplementation

Chronic fatigue is a debilitating condition that can affect every aspect of a person's life. This was the case for Mary, a 42-year-old woman who had been struggling with overwhelming fatigue for several years. Despite getting plenty of sleep and eating a reasonably balanced diet, Mary felt drained, lacked energy, and struggled to complete even the most basic daily tasks. Her fatigue was affecting her work, family life, and overall well-being.

Mary sought help from her primary care doctor, who ran blood tests to check her vitamin and mineral levels. The results showed that she was deficient in both magnesium and iron, two minerals that are essential for energy production. Magnesium plays a crucial role in ATP (adenosine triphosphate) production, the energy currency of cells, while iron is necessary for transporting oxygen to tissues through haemoglobin in red blood cells.

The doctor recommended a course of magnesium and iron supplementation. Mary began taking magnesium glycinate, a form known for its high bioavailability and minimal gastrointestinal side effects, along with ferrous sulfate, a standard form of iron supplementation. She also increased her intake of magnesium-rich foods like leafy greens, nuts, and seeds, as well as iron-rich foods such as lean red meat and spinach.

Within just a few weeks, Mary noticed a dramatic improvement in her energy levels. The fog of fatigue began to lift, and she found herself feeling more alert and motivated. She could now complete her workday without needing to rest, and her family noticed she had more energy to engage in activities she once enjoyed. Over time, her energy levels stabilised, and she was able to maintain her new vitality with continued supplementation and a nutrient-rich diet. Mary's story is a testament to how replenishing key minerals like magnesium and iron can reverse chronic fatigue and restore a person's quality of life.

Story 2: A Teenager Who Overcame Acne and Improved Immune Health with Zinc and Selenium

Acne is a common skin condition that affects millions of teenagers, but for 16-year-old James, it was more than just a few breakouts. His acne was severe, covering his face, neck, and back, and it had taken a toll on his self-esteem. In addition to his skin issues, James seemed to catch every cold and flu that went around, leading his parents to wonder if his immune system was compromised.

James visited a dermatologist, who prescribed topical treatments and antibiotics for his acne, but these provided only temporary relief and did not address the underlying issue. Eventually, his family sought out a nutritionist to explore whether there might be a nutritional deficiency contributing to both his acne and his poor immune health.

The nutritionist ordered blood tests and found that James had low levels of zinc and selenium—two minerals that are crucial for skin health and immune function. Zinc helps regulate oil production in the skin, reduces inflammation, and speeds up the healing process. Selenium, an antioxidant, helps protect skin cells from oxidative stress and supports immune function by boosting the body's ability to fight off infections.

The nutritionist recommended that James start supplementing with zinc picolinate, a form that is highly absorbable, along with selenium from Brazil nuts, which are one of the richest natural sources of selenium. James also made some dietary changes, increasing his intake of zinc-rich foods like shellfish, poultry, and legumes, and avoiding processed foods that could exacerbate his skin problems.

Within a few months, James saw a significant improvement in his skin. His acne breakouts became less frequent and less severe, and the inflammation in his skin subsided. His immune health also improved, and he noticed that he was no longer catching every cold that went around at school. By addressing his zinc and selenium deficiencies, James was able to clear up his skin and strengthen his immune system, giving him a new sense of confidence and well-being.

Story 3: Regaining Mobility and Bone Density with Calcium and Vitamin D

Osteoporosis is a condition that weakens bones and increases the risk of fractures, particularly in older adults. For John, a 72-year-old man, osteoporosis had started to take a toll on his quality of life. He experienced frequent aches and pains in his joints, and his mobility had become increasingly limited. John's fear of falling and suffering a serious injury made him hesitant to engage in physical activities that he once enjoyed, like gardening and walking his dog.

John's doctor diagnosed him with osteopenia, an early stage of osteoporosis, and recommended that he increase his intake of calcium and vitamin D. Both nutrients are essential for maintaining bone density. Calcium provides the structural material for bones, while vitamin D enhances calcium absorption in the intestines and helps regulate calcium levels in the blood.

John started taking a daily calcium supplement, along with vitamin D3, the most effective form of the vitamin for raising blood levels. His doctor also advised him to spend more time outdoors to boost his natural vitamin D production from sunlight and to include more calcium-rich foods like dairy products, fortified plant milks, and leafy greens in his diet.

Over the course of a year, John's bone density improved significantly, as confirmed by a follow-up DEXA scan (a test that measures bone density). More importantly, he regained much of his mobility and felt confident enough to return to his regular walks and outdoor activities. John's story highlights the importance of calcium and vitamin D in preventing and managing osteoporosis, allowing older adults to maintain an active lifestyle and reduce the risk of fractures.

Story 4: Reducing Anxiety and Improving Sleep with Magnesium and Potassium

Stress and anxiety are common problems in today's fast-paced world, and for 38-year-old David, the pressures of his demanding job were starting to take a toll on his mental health. David found himself feeling constantly anxious, and his sleep quality had deteriorated to the point where he was waking up multiple times during the night. He tried relaxation techniques and over-the-counter sleep aids, but nothing seemed to help.

David decided to visit a functional medicine practitioner, who took a holistic approach to his anxiety and sleep problems. After running a series of tests, the practitioner found that David had low levels of magnesium and potassium—two minerals that play a key role in regulating the nervous system and promoting restful sleep.

Magnesium is known for its calming effects on the nervous system, as it helps regulate neurotransmitters that influence mood and relaxation. Potassium, an essential electrolyte, supports muscle function and can help prevent muscle cramps or restless legs that might disturb sleep.

David began taking a nightly magnesium supplement in the form of magnesium citrate, which is easily absorbed and has a gentle relaxing effect. He also increased his intake of potassium-rich foods like bananas, sweet potatoes, and avocados. In addition, David worked on improving his sleep hygiene by reducing screen time before bed, keeping his bedroom cool and dark, and establishing a regular sleep schedule.

Within a few weeks, David noticed a significant reduction in his anxiety levels. He felt calmer throughout the day and was able to manage work-related stress more effectively. His sleep also improved dramatically—he was falling asleep faster and staying asleep through the night, waking up feeling refreshed and energised.

By addressing his magnesium and potassium deficiencies, David was able to break the cycle of anxiety and poor sleep, improving both his mental health and his quality of life. His case demonstrates the powerful connection between minerals, stress regulation, and sleep quality.

Conclusion

These case histories illustrate the profound impact that mineral supplementation can have on various aspects of health. Whether it's reversing chronic fatigue with magnesium and iron, clearing up acne and boosting immune health with zinc and selenium, improving bone density and mobility with calcium and vitamin D, or reducing anxiety and improving sleep with magnesium and potassium, mineral replenishment can transform lives.

While it's always important to work with healthcare professionals to identify deficiencies and develop a personalised supplementation plan, these stories show that targeted mineral replenishment can offer a natural and effective solution to many common health challenges. By ensuring that the body has the essential minerals it needs, individuals can experience significant improvements in their energy levels, immune function, bone health, and overall well-being.

Summary: Case Histories – The Miracles of Mineral Replenishment

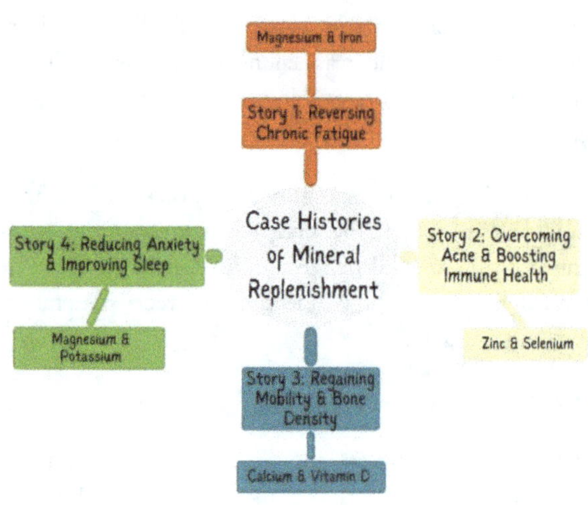

Chapter 9
The Future of Mineral Therapy – Personalised Nutrition and Prevention

As our understanding of nutrition and health deepens, the role of minerals in maintaining optimal health is becoming increasingly clear. Far from being simply building blocks for bones and muscles, minerals play vital roles in nearly every physiological process, from regulating heart function to maintaining cognitive health. As we look to the future of mineral therapy, the focus is shifting towards personalised nutrition—tailoring mineral supplementation to individual needs to prevent chronic diseases, enhance performance, and promote long-term health and longevity.

Minerals in Chronic Disease Prevention

Minerals are fundamental to preventing chronic diseases that are prevalent in modern societies. Deficiencies in essential minerals like magnesium, calcium, and trace elements such as selenium and zinc have been linked to a host of conditions, including heart disease, osteoporosis, and diabetes. Ensuring adequate intake of these minerals can be a powerful tool for disease prevention.

Magnesium and Heart Disease

Magnesium is involved in over 300 enzymatic reactions in the body, many of which are critical for cardiovascular health. Low magnesium levels have been associated with an increased risk of heart disease, hypertension, and arrhythmias. Magnesium helps regulate blood pressure by relaxing blood vessels, supporting healthy heart rhythms, and preventing the buildup of calcium in arterial walls, which can lead to hardening of the arteries (atherosclerosis).

Studies show that individuals with higher magnesium intake tend to have lower rates of heart disease. Magnesium supplementation has been found to reduce blood pressure, improve heart function, and lower the risk of heart attacks and strokes. As more people seek non-pharmacological ways to support heart health, magnesium supplementation is likely to play a key role in cardiovascular disease prevention in the future.

Calcium and Osteoporosis

Calcium is essential for maintaining strong bones and preventing osteoporosis, a condition that affects millions of people worldwide, particularly postmenopausal women and the elderly. Adequate calcium intake, combined with vitamin D, helps preserve bone density and reduce the risk of fractures. As we age, our ability to absorb calcium from the diet decreases, making supplementation a critical strategy for osteoporosis prevention.

Calcium is also involved in muscle function, nerve transmission, and blood clotting. Ensuring sufficient calcium intake through diet or supplementation can help maintain mobility and independence in older adults by reducing the likelihood of falls and fractures.

Trace Minerals and Diabetes

Trace minerals like chromium, zinc, and selenium play important roles in regulating blood sugar and preventing metabolic disorders such as type 2 diabetes. Chromium enhances the action of insulin, the hormone responsible for regulating blood sugar levels. Studies have shown that chromium supplementation can improve glucose tolerance and reduce insulin resistance, making it a valuable tool for managing and preventing diabetes.

Zinc is also important for insulin production and secretion, while selenium's antioxidant properties help protect pancreatic cells from oxidative stress, which can lead to insulin dysfunction. By ensuring adequate intake of these trace minerals, individuals can support healthy blood sugar regulation and reduce the risk of developing diabetes.

Biohacking and Performance: Optimising Physical and Mental Performance with Personalised Mineral Supplementation

The growing field of biohacking is driving a new era of personalised mineral supplementation. Biohackers—individuals who experiment with diet, supplements, and lifestyle interventions to optimise their health—are increasingly using minerals to enhance both physical and mental performance. Personalised mineral therapy is at the forefront of this movement, offering tailored solutions to improve endurance, cognitive function, and recovery.

Magnesium for Performance and Recovery

Magnesium is one of the most popular minerals in biohacking circles, particularly for its role in muscle function, energy production, and recovery. Athletes and fitness enthusiasts often use magnesium supplementation to prevent muscle cramps, improve endurance, and enhance post-exercise recovery. Magnesium helps regulate muscle contractions and reduces the buildup of lactic acid, which can lead to muscle soreness.

In addition to its physical benefits, magnesium has a profound effect on mental performance. It plays a key role in neurotransmitter function and stress regulation, making it a popular supplement for individuals looking to improve focus, reduce anxiety, and enhance sleep quality. By replenishing magnesium stores, biohackers can optimise both their physical and cognitive abilities.

Potassium and Sodium for Electrolyte Balance

Electrolyte balance is critical for maintaining optimal hydration, nerve function, and muscle performance. Potassium and sodium work together to regulate fluid balance and electrical impulses in the body. Biohackers often use potassium supplements or electrolyte drinks to maintain proper hydration during intense physical activity, which helps prevent muscle cramps, fatigue, and dehydration.

For individuals engaged in endurance sports, balancing sodium and potassium is essential to preventing hyponatremia (low sodium levels), a condition that can occur when too much water is consumed without adequate sodium intake. By fine-tuning their electrolyte intake, biohackers can optimise their performance and reduce the risk of dehydration-related complications.

Zinc and Selenium for Cognitive Function

Zinc and selenium are increasingly recognised for their role in cognitive health and mental performance. Zinc is involved in neurotransmitter function and plays a role in memory formation and learning. Deficiencies in zinc have been linked to cognitive decline and conditions such as depression and Alzheimer's disease.

Selenium, an antioxidant mineral, helps protect brain cells from oxidative damage and supports thyroid function, which is important for maintaining cognitive function. Biohackers who focus on enhancing mental clarity and preventing cognitive decline often use zinc and selenium supplements as part of their personalised nutrition strategies.

Emerging Research: Trace Minerals in Mental Health, Gut Health, and Longevity

As research into minerals continues to expand, new insights are emerging about the role of trace minerals in mental health, gut health, and longevity. These findings are paving the way for more targeted mineral therapies aimed at preventing disease and promoting long-term health.

Trace Minerals and Mental Health

Emerging research suggests that trace minerals such as zinc, magnesium, and copper play a significant role in mental health. Zinc and magnesium are particularly important for regulating mood and reducing anxiety. Low levels of these minerals have been linked to depression, anxiety, and other mental health disorders.

For example, studies have shown that zinc supplementation can improve symptoms of depression, particularly when combined with antidepressant medications. Magnesium has also been found to have mood-stabilising effects, and its use as a natural treatment for anxiety and depression is growing.

Copper, another trace mineral, is essential for the production of neurotransmitters like dopamine and serotonin, which regulate mood and emotion. However, imbalances in copper levels can lead to mood disorders, highlighting the importance of maintaining proper mineral balance for mental health.

Trace Minerals and Gut Health

The gut microbiome is increasingly recognised as a key player in overall health, and trace minerals are crucial for supporting gut health. Zinc, for example, helps maintain the integrity of the gut lining and supports the healing of intestinal damage. Magnesium is involved in smooth muscle function in the digestive tract, helping to regulate bowel movements and prevent constipation.

Selenium's antioxidant properties help reduce inflammation in the gut, which is important for preventing conditions like irritable bowel syndrome (IBS) and leaky gut syndrome. As the connection between the gut and the brain (the gut-brain axis) continues to be explored, it's becoming clear that trace minerals play a vital role in maintaining a healthy gut microbiome, which in turn supports mental health, immune function, and overall well-being.

Trace Minerals and Longevity

The role of trace minerals in promoting longevity is a growing area of research. Minerals like selenium, zinc, and magnesium have powerful antioxidant properties that help protect cells from oxidative damage, one of the key factors in ageing. By reducing oxidative stress and inflammation, trace minerals can help prevent age-related diseases and promote healthy ageing.

Selenium, in particular, has been studied for its role in extending lifespan. Animal studies have shown that selenium supplementation can increase longevity by enhancing the body's ability to repair DNA and reduce oxidative damage. In humans, selenium has been linked to a reduced risk of age-related diseases such as Alzheimer's and cardiovascular disease.

Magnesium's role in preventing chronic diseases like heart disease, diabetes, and osteoporosis also makes it a key mineral for promoting longevity. By supporting bone health, cardiovascular function, and metabolic health, magnesium helps individuals maintain vitality and independence as they age.

The Future of Personalised Mineral Therapy

The future of mineral therapy lies in personalisation—tailoring supplementation to an individual's unique genetic makeup, lifestyle, and health status. Advances in technology, such as genetic testing and personalised nutrition platforms, are making it easier to identify specific mineral deficiencies and develop customised supplementation plans.

For example, nutrigenomics (the study of how genes interact with nutrients) is helping researchers understand how individual genetic variations affect mineral metabolism. This knowledge allows for more precise recommendations based on a person's genetic predisposition to certain deficiencies or diseases.

Wearable health devices and apps that monitor nutrient intake, physical activity, and health markers are also contributing to the rise of personalised mineral therapy. These tools allow individuals to track their mineral levels and adjust their supplementation in real-time, ensuring that they receive the optimal amount of minerals for their health goals.

In the future, personalised mineral therapy will likely become an integral part of preventive medicine, helping individuals optimise their mineral intake to prevent disease, enhance performance, and promote longevity.

Conclusion

Minerals are essential for preventing chronic diseases, optimising performance, and promoting long-term health and well-being. As research continues to uncover the critical roles that minerals play in mental health, gut health, and longevity, personalised mineral therapy is emerging as a powerful tool for preventive health.

By tailoring mineral supplementation to individual needs, we can address deficiencies before they lead to chronic diseases, enhance physical and mental performance, and support healthy ageing. As personalised nutrition continues to evolve, minerals will undoubtedly play a central role in the future of preventive medicine and wellness.

Summary: The Future of Mineral Therapy – Personalised Nutrition and Prevention

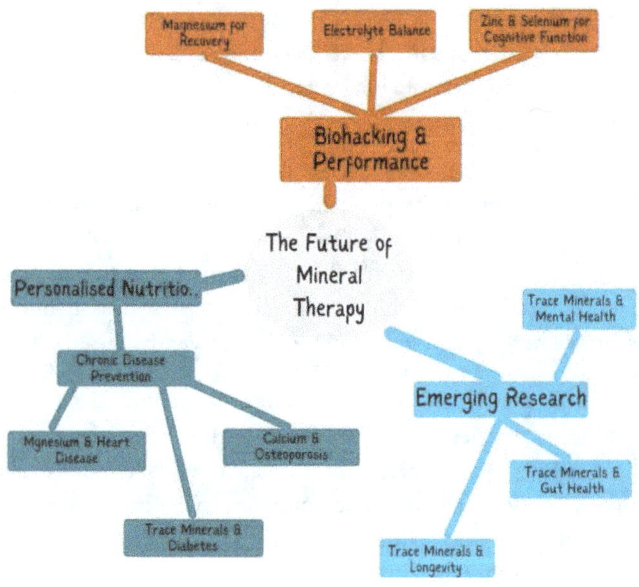

Chapter 10
Conclusion
Reclaiming Our Health Through Mineral Replenishment

Minerals are often overlooked in conversations about nutrition, but they are as vital to health as vitamins, proteins, and carbohydrates. These essential nutrients serve as the foundational building blocks that regulate everything from bone density to heart function, muscle health, and brain activity. Yet, modern lifestyles, characterised by processed foods, poor soil quality, and the stresses of daily life, have led to widespread mineral deficiencies. In this conclusion, we will recap the critical role of minerals in health and discuss how addressing these deficiencies through dietary improvements, oral supplementation, and IV therapy can empower individuals to reclaim their health and improve their quality of life.

Recap: The Critical Role of Minerals in Health

Throughout this book, we have explored the profound impact that minerals have on every aspect of human health. Minerals are not just passive components of the diet; they are active participants in countless biochemical processes essential for survival and well-being. Let's revisit some of the key ways that minerals contribute to optimal health and the prevention of chronic diseases.

1. **Energy Production and Metabolism**: Magnesium, iron, and other trace minerals are vital for energy production at the cellular level. Magnesium is involved in ATP synthesis, the energy currency of the cell, while iron is necessary for oxygen transport, ensuring that the body's tissues receive the fuel they need for energy metabolism. Without sufficient levels of these

minerals, individuals can experience fatigue, sluggishness, and a range of metabolic disorders.

2. **Bone and Muscle Health**: Calcium and magnesium are two of the most important minerals for bone health, working in tandem to maintain bone density and prevent osteoporosis. Adequate calcium intake is essential for strong bones, while magnesium ensures that calcium is effectively absorbed and utilised. In addition, potassium and sodium help regulate muscle contractions and nerve signals, reducing the risk of muscle cramps, weakness, and even cardiovascular issues.

3. **Cardiovascular Health**: Heart disease is the leading cause of death worldwide, and mineral deficiencies are a major contributing factor. Magnesium, calcium, and potassium play a critical role in maintaining heart rhythm, regulating blood pressure, and preventing arterial calcification. Ensuring optimal intake of these minerals is essential for maintaining cardiovascular health and reducing the risk of heart attacks, strokes, and hypertension.

4. **Mental Health and Cognitive Function**: The connection between minerals and mental health is often overlooked, but deficiencies in key minerals like zinc, magnesium, and selenium have been linked to mood disorders, cognitive decline, and even neurodegenerative diseases like Alzheimer's. Zinc and magnesium are crucial for neurotransmitter function, while selenium acts as a powerful antioxidant that protects brain cells from oxidative stress.

5. **Immune System Support**: Trace minerals such as zinc, selenium, and copper are essential for a healthy immune system. Zinc helps the body produce immune cells that fight infections, while selenium's antioxidant properties protect against inflammation and infection. Adequate intake of these minerals can boost the body's natural defences, helping to ward off illness and accelerate recovery.

6. **Chronic Disease Prevention**: Beyond specific functions, minerals play a preventive role in chronic diseases like diabetes, osteoporosis, and heart disease. Chromium supports insulin function, which is critical for blood sugar regulation and diabetes prevention, while calcium and magnesium are vital for preventing osteoporosis and maintaining bone health. By ensuring optimal mineral intake, individuals can reduce their risk of developing these and other chronic diseases, promoting long-term health and vitality.

Addressing Modern Mineral Deficiencies

In today's world, where processed foods dominate and modern agricultural practices deplete soil of its nutrients, it's no surprise that mineral deficiencies are widespread. Many individuals are simply not getting the essential minerals they need from their diet alone. The consequences of these deficiencies can range from mild symptoms like fatigue and muscle cramps to serious conditions like osteoporosis, heart disease, and cognitive decline. However, the good news is that these deficiencies are both preventable and reversible.

To reclaim our health, we must focus on three key strategies for addressing mineral deficiencies: **dietary improvements**, **oral supplementation**, and **IV therapy**.

1. Dietary Improvements

The first step in addressing mineral deficiencies is to prioritise a nutrient-dense diet. Whole, unprocessed foods are the best sources of minerals, as they provide a variety of essential nutrients in their natural forms. By making simple adjustments to our daily diet, we can significantly improve our mineral intake.

- **Magnesium-rich foods**: Leafy green vegetables like spinach, kale, and Swiss chard, as well as nuts, seeds, and whole grains, are excellent sources of magnesium. Adding these foods to your meals can help prevent magnesium deficiency, which is common in modern diets.

- **Calcium-rich foods**: Dairy products such as milk, yoghurt, and cheese are well-known sources of calcium, but plant-based options like fortified plant milks, tofu, and leafy greens also provide calcium. Including a variety of these foods ensures strong bones and prevents osteoporosis.

- **Iron-rich foods**: Red meat, poultry, and fish are excellent sources of heme iron, which is easily absorbed by the body. Plant-based sources of non-heme iron, like lentils, beans, and spinach, should be paired with vitamin C-rich foods (such as citrus fruits or bell peppers) to enhance absorption.

- **Zinc and selenium-rich foods**: Shellfish, seeds, nuts, and Brazil nuts are rich in zinc and selenium, both of which are important for immune function and cognitive health. Incorporating these into your diet can help support overall wellness.

By focusing on a varied and balanced diet that includes plenty of mineral-rich foods, individuals can take a proactive approach to preventing deficiencies and maintaining optimal health.

2. Oral Supplementation

While dietary improvements are important, there are times when diet alone is not enough to meet the body's mineral needs. This is especially true for individuals with specific health conditions, dietary restrictions, or lifestyles that increase their mineral requirements. In these cases, oral supplementation can be a valuable tool for ensuring adequate mineral intake.

- **Magnesium supplements**: Magnesium is one of the most common mineral deficiencies, and supplements such as magnesium glycinate or citrate are highly bioavailable forms that are gentle on the digestive system. These supplements can help alleviate symptoms of magnesium deficiency, such as muscle cramps, fatigue, and anxiety.

- **Calcium and vitamin D supplements**: For individuals at risk of osteoporosis or those who do not consume enough calcium through their diet, calcium supplements (preferably calcium citrate, which is easier to absorb) can be paired with vitamin D to enhance calcium absorption and support bone health.

- **Zinc and selenium supplements**: Zinc picolinate and selenium supplements are particularly beneficial for immune support and cognitive health, especially during times of illness or stress when the body's need for these minerals increases.

- **Iron supplements**: For individuals with iron deficiency anaemia, iron supplements such as ferrous sulfate or iron bisglycinate can help restore healthy iron levels and improve energy and cognitive function.

Oral supplementation allows for targeted and controlled mineral intake, ensuring that the body receives the exact nutrients it needs to correct deficiencies and maintain optimal health.

3. IV Therapy

In some cases, oral supplementation may not be sufficient, particularly for individuals with gut absorption issues or those who need rapid replenishment of minerals. For these individuals, **IV mineral therapy** offers a fast and effective solution. By delivering minerals directly into the bloodstream, IV therapy bypasses the digestive system, ensuring 100% absorption and immediate availability to the body.

- **Magnesium IV therapy**: Individuals with severe magnesium deficiencies, athletes requiring quick recovery, or those experiencing chronic stress can benefit from magnesium IV drips, which rapidly restore magnesium levels and promote relaxation, improved muscle function, and stress relief.

- **Multi-mineral IV therapy**: For individuals with multiple mineral deficiencies or those looking to optimise their overall wellness, multi-mineral IV drips provide a comprehensive solution. These drips typically contain a blend of essential minerals, including magnesium, calcium, zinc, selenium, and others, tailored to the individual's needs.

IV mineral therapy is particularly useful for people recovering from surgery, chronic illness, or intense physical exertion, as it provides an immediate boost of essential nutrients that can accelerate healing, improve energy levels, and enhance overall well-being.

Final Thoughts: Reclaiming Our Health Through Mineral Replenishment

In a world where modern lifestyles have made mineral deficiencies all too common, addressing these deficiencies is not just an option—it is a necessity for optimal health and well-being. Minerals are the foundation upon which the body's physiological processes are built, and ensuring adequate intake is key to preventing chronic diseases, enhancing mental and physical performance, and promoting longevity.

By making dietary improvements, incorporating targeted oral supplementation, and utilising IV therapy when necessary, we can take control of our health and replenish the minerals that our bodies need to thrive. Whether through the foods we eat, the supplements we take, or the treatments we choose, mineral replenishment offers a simple yet powerful path to better health, increased energy, and a higher quality of life.

As we move forward in understanding the critical role of minerals in health, it's clear that reclaiming our well-being through mineral replenishment is not just a trend—it is a return to the basics of what the human body requires to function optimally. By embracing the power of minerals, we can unlock our full potential and live healthier, more vibrant lives.

Summary: Conclusion
Reclaiming Our Health Through Mineral Replenishment

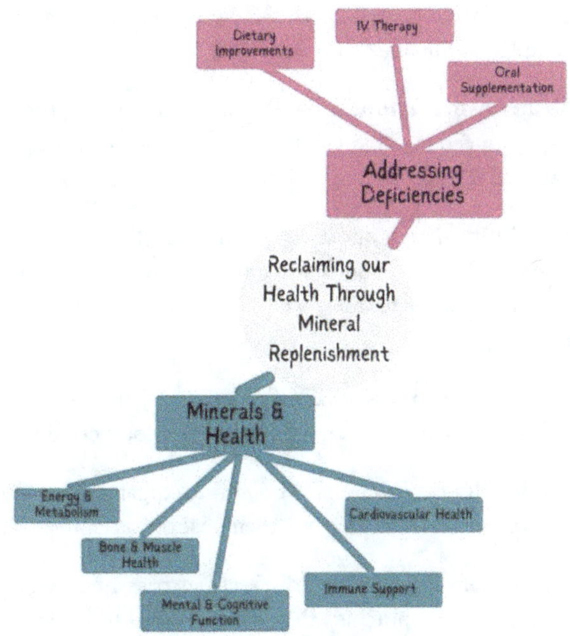

Glossary

1. **Anaemia**: A condition often caused by iron deficiency, characterised by fatigue, weakness, and pale skin, due to reduced oxygen-carrying capacity of the blood.

2. **Antioxidant**: A substance that inhibits oxidation, protecting cells from damage caused by free radicals. Selenium and zinc are examples of minerals with antioxidant properties.

3. **ATP (Adenosine Triphosphate)**: The main energy currency of cells, produced through biochemical reactions involving key minerals such as magnesium and phosphorus.

4. **Bioavailability**: The proportion of a nutrient that is absorbed and used by the body. In mineral supplementation, bioavailability refers to how well the body can absorb and utilise the mineral.

5. **Calcium**: A mineral essential for building strong bones and teeth, muscle function, nerve signalling, and blood clotting.

6. **Chelated Minerals**: Minerals bound to organic molecules (such as amino acids) to improve their absorption in the body.

7. **Chronic Disease**: Long-term diseases, such as heart disease, diabetes, and osteoporosis, that often result from lifestyle factors, including poor nutrition and mineral deficiencies.

8. **Depleted Soil**: Soil that has lost its natural mineral content due to modern agricultural practices, leading to reduced mineral content in food crops.

9. **Electrolytes**: Minerals such as sodium, potassium, and magnesium that regulate fluid balance, nerve function, and muscle contractions.

10. **Fatigue**: A common symptom of mineral deficiency, particularly involving magnesium, iron, and potassium, where an individual experiences extreme tiredness or lack of energy.

11. **Ferrous Sulfate**: A common form of iron supplement used to treat and prevent iron deficiency anaemia.

12. **Gut Absorption**: The process by which nutrients, including minerals, are absorbed in the intestines and transferred into the bloodstream for use by the body.

13. **Heme Iron**: The form of iron found in animal products, which is more easily absorbed by the body compared to non-heme iron found in plants.

14. **Hypochlorhydria**: A condition characterised by low stomach acid, which can impair the absorption of minerals such as calcium and magnesium.

15. **Insulin Resistance**: A condition where the body's cells become less responsive to insulin, often leading to type 2 diabetes. Minerals like magnesium and chromium help regulate blood sugar and insulin function.

16. **Iron**: A vital mineral that helps produce haemoglobin in red blood cells, allowing oxygen to be carried throughout the body.

17. **IV (Intravenous) Mineral Therapy**: The delivery of minerals directly into the bloodstream through a drip, bypassing the digestive system for immediate absorption.

18. **Magnesium**: An essential mineral involved in over 300 enzymatic reactions, including energy production, muscle relaxation, and nerve function.

19. **Mineral Deficiency**: A condition where the body lacks adequate levels of essential minerals, leading to various health

problems, such as fatigue, poor bone health, and immune dysfunction.

20. **Mineral Replenishment**: The process of restoring adequate levels of minerals in the body through dietary improvements, supplementation, or IV therapy.

21. **Multimineral Supplement**: A dietary supplement containing a combination of essential minerals, often used to correct deficiencies or support overall health.

22. **Neurotransmitters**: Chemicals in the brain that transmit signals between nerve cells. Minerals like magnesium and zinc are involved in neurotransmitter function, affecting mood and cognition.

23. **Osteoporosis**: A disease characterised by weak and brittle bones, often due to calcium and vitamin D deficiencies.

24. **Oxidative Stress**: An imbalance between free radicals and antioxidants in the body, leading to cell damage. Antioxidant minerals like selenium and zinc help mitigate oxidative stress.

25. **Potassium**: A mineral crucial for maintaining proper heart function, fluid balance, and muscle contractions.

26. **Restoration Therapy**: A treatment approach focused on replenishing the body's minerals and nutrients to restore health and prevent disease.

27. **Selenium**: A trace mineral with powerful antioxidant properties that support immune function and protect cells from oxidative stress.

28. **Trace Minerals**: Minerals needed in small amounts for various biochemical processes in the body, such as zinc, selenium, and copper.

29. **Vitamin D**: A fat-soluble vitamin essential for calcium absorption and bone health. It also supports immune function and is produced when the skin is exposed to sunlight.

30. **Zinc**: A mineral important for immune function, wound healing, DNA synthesis, and skin health.

References

- Abbasi J. "Magnesium: Broadening the Cardiometabolic Evidence Base." JAMA, 2019.

- Ali H, Weiler H, Atkinson SA. "Calcium supplementation to prevent and treat osteoporosis in postmenopausal women." Journal of Clinical Endocrinology & Metabolism, 2010.

- Bailey RL, et al. "The epidemiology of global micronutrient deficiencies." Advances in Nutrition, 2015.

- Bailey RL, West KP Jr, Black RE. "The epidemiology of global micronutrient deficiencies." Annals of Nutrition and Metabolism, 2015.

- Barbagallo M, Dominguez LJ. "Magnesium and ageing." Current Pharmaceutical Design, 2010.

- Berkemeyer S, et al. "Plasma magnesium status and dietary intake in different populations." Journal of Clinical Endocrinology and Metabolism, 2011.

- Berridge MJ. "Vitamin D deficiency and diabetes." Biochemical Journal, 2017.

- Berridge MJ. "Vitamin D, reactive oxygen species and calcium signalling in ageing and disease." Trends in Cell Biology, 2020.

- Broadley MR, White PJ, Hammond JP, et al. "Zinc in plants." New Phytologist, 2007.

- Brown EM. "Calcium and bone health: What's the evidence?" Clinical Cases in Mineral and Bone Metabolism, 2015.

- Bryant MJ, Dreher ML. "Bioavailability of minerals in whole foods versus supplements." Journal of Nutrition, 2015.

- Cannata-Andía JB, et al. "Secondary hyperparathyroidism: pathogenesis, disease progression, and therapeutic options." Clinical Journal of the American Society of Nephrology, 2012.

- Cappuccio FP, Kalaitzidis R, Duneclift S, et al. "Unraveling the links between calcium, potassium, magnesium, and cardiovascular diseases." Hypertension, 2006.

- Choi YJ, Chung YS. "The Role of Vitamin D and Calcium in Bone Health and Osteoporosis." Journal of Bone Metabolism, 2020.

- Clark SF. "Iron deficiency anaemia." Nutrition in Clinical Practice, 2008.

- Cooper C, Harvey N. "Vitamin D and the prevention of osteoporotic fractures." Osteoporosis International, 2016.

- DiNicolantonio JJ, O'Keefe JH, Wilson W. "Subclinical magnesium deficiency: A principal driver of cardiovascular disease and a public health crisis." Open Heart, 2018.

- Dominguez LJ, Barbagallo M. "The significance of magnesium in metabolic disorders and ageing." Biological Trace Element Research, 2010.

- Drake MT, Clarke BL, Lewiecki EM. "The pathophysiology and treatment of osteoporosis." Clinical Therapeutics, 2015.

- Dror DK, Allen LH. "Effect of vitamin B12 deficiency on neurodevelopment in infants: current knowledge and possible mechanisms." Nutrition Reviews, 2008.

- García OP, Long KZ, Rosado JL. "Impact of micronutrient deficiencies on obesity." Nutrition Reviews, 2009.

- Grant WB. "A review of the role of solar ultraviolet-B irradiance and vitamin D in reducing the risk of chronic diseases." Public Health Nutrition, 2007.

- Gropper SS, Smith JL, Groff JL. "Advanced Nutrition and Human Metabolism." Cengage Learning, 2012.

- Hart PH, Gorman S, Finlay-Jones JJ. "Modulation of the immune system by UV radiation: more than just the effects of vitamin D?" Nature Reviews Immunology, 2011.

- Institute of Medicine. "Dietary Reference Intakes for Calcium and Vitamin D." National Academies Press, 2011.

- Kaplowitz N. "Biochemistry and liver toxicity of iron." Seminars in Liver Disease, 2014.

- Kaur J, et al. "Dietary intake of trace elements and minerals." Nutrients, 2019.

- Kilic E, Kilic U, Reiter RJ, et al. "Melatonin in neurological diseases: protective effects via mitochondrial regulation." Journal of Pineal Research, 2009.

- Kulczyński B, Gramza-Michałowska A. "The role of selenium in human health and chronic diseases." Journal of Nutrition, 2017.

- Lee BJ, Lin JS, Lin YC. "Role of trace elements in cardiovascular diseases." Journal of Biomedicine and Biotechnology, 2012.

- Lukaski HC. "Vitamin and mineral status: effects on physical performance." Nutrition, 2004.

- Malavolta M, et al. "Trace elements in ageing and Alzheimer's disease." Mechanisms of Ageing and Development, 2016.

- Maret W. "Zinc biochemistry: from a single zinc enzyme to a key element of life." Advances in Nutrition, 2013.

- Marfella R, Paolisso G. "Sodium-potassium balance and cardiovascular disease: New therapeutic targets." Hypertension, 2021.

- Mozaffarian D, et al. "Magnesium and cardiovascular health." Circulation Research, 2018.

- Mursu J, Voutilainen S, Nurmi T. "Dietary intakes and serum concentrations of selenium in men with and without coronary heart disease." British Journal of Nutrition, 2014.

- Nasri H, Rafieian-Kopaei M. "Metformin: Current knowledge." Journal of Research in Medical Sciences, 2014.

- National Institutes of Health (NIH). "Iron: Fact Sheet for Health Professionals." NIH Office of Dietary Supplements, 2021.

- Nielsen FH. "Magnesium deficiency and increased inflammation: Current perspectives." Journal of Inflammation Research, 2018.

- O'Neil C, Hoffman RP. "Role of magnesium in insulin action, diabetes, and cardio-metabolic syndrome X." Magnesium Research, 2012.

- Olivares M, et al. "Iron, zinc, and copper: deficiencies and the role of trace minerals in immune function." The American Journal of Clinical Nutrition, 2020.

- Pittas AG, Dawson-Hughes B. "Vitamin D and diabetes." The Journal of Steroid Biochemistry and Molecular Biology, 2010.

- Powell JJ, Whitehead MW, Ainley CC, et al. "Dietary minerals in health and disease: the impact of dietary mineral bioavailability on disease processes." Clinical Science, 2017.

- Prasad AS. "Zinc in human health: effect of zinc on immune cells." Molecular Medicine, 2008.

- Prentice A. "Calcium in nutrition and health: an overview." Nutrition Bulletin, 2012.

- Prentice AM, Ghattas H, Cox SE. "Host-pathogen interactions: can micronutrients tip the balance?" The Journal of Nutrition, 2007.

- Razzaque MS. "FGF23, klotho and vitamin D interactions: what role in human ageing?" Ageing Research Reviews, 2018.

- Reddy V, Sivakumar B. "Magnesium metabolism in health and disease." Clinical Biochemistry, 2016.

- Reffitt DM, Ogston N, Jugdaohsingh R, et al. "Orthosilicic acid stimulates collagen type 1 synthesis and osteoblastic differentiation in human osteoblast-like cells in vitro." Bone, 2003.

- Samman S. "Zinc supplementation and bone turnover in healthy men." Journal of Bone and Mineral Research, 2010.

- Scott D, Blizzard L, Fell J, et al. "A prospective study of the role of muscle strength, physical activity, and dietary calcium in the prevention of falls in older people." Journal of Bone and Mineral Research, 2011.

- Seeman E, Martin TJ. "Coordinated pathways controlling skeletal health: Novel approaches to prevention and treatment of bone fragility." Journal of Bone and Mineral Research, 2019.

- Sharif R, Thomas P, Holt T. "The Role of Selenium in Thyroid Gland Function and Pathophysiology." Hormones, 2020.

- Skalny AV, et al. "Zinc deficiency as a mediator of cognitive impairment and depression in the elderly." International Journal of Molecular Sciences, 2021.

- Skalny AV, et al. "Zinc deficiency as a mediator of cognitive impairment and depression in the elderly." International Journal of Molecular Sciences, 2021.

- Traber MG. "The role of vitamin E in antioxidant defence." The American Journal of Clinical Nutrition, 2007.

- Weaver CM, Alexander DD, Boushey CJ, et al. "Calcium plus vitamin D supplementation and risk of fractures: an updated meta-analysis from the National Osteoporosis Foundation." Osteoporosis International, 2016.

- Weaver CM, Heaney RP. "Calcium in human health." Humana Press, 2006.

- World Health Organization (WHO). "Guidelines on calcium and magnesium in drinking water." WHO, 2011.

- Zimmermann MB, Boelaert K. "Iodine deficiency and thyroid disorders." Lancet Diabetes Endocrinology, 2015.

www.ingramcontent.com/pod-product-compliance
Lightning Source LLC
Chambersburg PA
CBHW070410200726

48294CB00003B/1148